Spirited Blend

A Paramour Bay Mystery
Book Nine

KENNEDY LAYNE

DEDICATION

Jeffrey—Your homemade smoking cauldron for this year's Halloween display should be sold in stores...I love you!

Cole—You're the best horror movie partner a mother could ask for!

Get ready for a spine-tingling cozy mystery that has ghosts, ghouls, and goblins coming out of the woodwork in the next spirited installment of the Paramour Bay Mysteries by USA Today Bestselling Author Kennedy Layne...

Mounds of delicious candy corn, jack-o-lanterns, and spooky hayrides are all part of this year's Halloween festivities in Paramour Bay. Raven Marigold plans to make the most out of this All Hallows' Eve, which just so happens to be her birthday.

Not everyone in town seems to have gotten the festive memo, though. One of the residents is claiming that the spirit of her dead husband has been paying her nocturnal visits, while other townsfolk are making similar claims about their deceased relatives. Is this someone's version of a supernatural flash mob or has someone accidentally pierced the veil to the afterlife?

It's going to be a hauntingly good time in this quaint coastal town, so bring along your lanterns and flashlights as Raven and the gang take a midnight stroll through the local cemetery to try and solve this hair-raising mystery!

Chapter One

"**I**S THERE A reason that you and Leo both look like two of the walking dead?"

I blinked rapidly, wondering if I had any eye drops in the junk drawer below the cash register. I'd gotten in the habit of keeping it full of useful items, though I never seemed to have on hand what I needed at the moment. The zombie guise wasn't exactly what I was going for in the hair and makeup department for this All Hallows' Eve.

I called it All Hallows' Eve and not Halloween in deference to the sacred holiday, and not the commercial boondoggle the sugar industry had made it in recent years. Not that I turned away any candy treats that were filled with one of my favorite substances. With that said, I was prepared as any self-respecting witch could be in this day and age.

My tasteful witch's costume was currently hanging in my closet, ready to wear tomorrow for the big social event—the town's extravagant trick or treating shindig. What I needed more than anything right now was coffee, and copious amounts at that.

Go ahead. Tell Heidi that doomsday has finally arrived with the vengeance of a comet streaking across the night sky. We might as well say our final goodbyes.

"The cesaral spirit bell might have rung again last night," I reluctantly shared with Heidi Connolly before walking over to the convenient coffee sampling station I'd set up inside the tea shop a few months ago.

I couldn't deny that I had ulterior motives with such an elaborate display of three different flavors prepared in pump still urns, odd as that condition might seem for someone who is in fact the owner of the town's only tea and specialty gourmet tea shop.

Bottom line?

Coffee was my sanity.

"That makes five times the bell has signaled the presence of a spirit since August. Does that mean one spirit has visited Paramour Bay five times, or does it mean that five spirits are roaming around town without anyone being the wiser? I don't like it, Heidi. Not one bit."

You don't like it? This cesaral spirit bell is ruining my life. Did you forget that it's October? Skippy and his merry band of ninja squirrels are preparing for their winter hibernation, and I haven't once put so much as a hitch into their well-thought out survival plans. What kind of nemesis does that make me? Pitiful.

"Isn't it possible that spirits who haven't crossed through the veil roam around us every single day without any of us knowing they are an arm's width away?" Heidi asked perceptively, tucking one of her many blonde curls behind her ears as she handed me a fresh cup of hot Columbian Supremo coffee. A best friend always knew what the other needed. "Nothing bad has happened since you came into possession of all those lost occult items that you and Leo discovered at the antique shop. It's time for you to return to the land of the living…no pun intended."

Does my Heidi not understand the "point of no return" saying? You should jog her memory before we're inundated with evil spirits bent on destroying the town. Possession is nothing to sneeze at, you know.

The voice inside my head belonged to my one and only magical familiar—Leo, the cat. Technically, he used to be my grandmother's familiar, but I'd sort of inherited him due to a necromancy spell gone awry. Don't get me wrong. The spell worked, just with some rather inconvenient consequences.

Now might be a good time to for me introduce myself.

My name is Raven Lattice Marigold, and I'm a bona fide honest to goodness witch. I've had some growing pains in the spell department, but I was getting better with time and experience dealing with what I believed to be the illogical twists and turns of the craft.

Honestly?

I absolutely loved being a witch, and also knowing the existence of the supernatural.

Thinking back over the past year since my Nan had passed away, I was really proud of how far I'd come both professionally and personally as an adult. I'd gone from being a naïve receptionist living in the Big Apple to becoming a small business owner creating a home here in the quaint, coastal town of Paramour Bay, Connecticut. I was no longer unattached, even though I had more confidence in who I was as an independent woman than ever before.

We were currently inside my tea shop, given that it was a Wednesday at eight-thirty in the morning. *Tea, Leaves, & Eves* was the name of the charming store my Nan had established fifty-four years ago. The town itself was very Norman Rockwell-esque, reflected in the attractive cobblestone intersections and charming wrought iron café tables which sat in the shade of the numerous trees dotted along the wide sidewalk in front of various shops, including mine. In all actuality, the tables belonged to the town's parks department and they were collected for storage when the fall weather turned, signaling the end of our summer tourism season.

As for the tea shop itself, gold tassels hung from the awning outside, while the plate glass display window appeared to be a century old; the waves and bubbled appearance highlighting its unique, tiny imperfections. I had strategically placed a few high-top tables around the shop for my customers to sample the specialty blends, with one specific area dedicated for my sanity-saving drink. The other four fifths of the shelves were lined with delicate porcelain teacups, light blue tinted glass containers of various tea leaves, and the accessories that went into the time-consuming task of making the most delicious brew for any tea lover. In the midst of all of the inventory were small keepsake trinkets however loosely related to the tea and coffee trade from various parts of the world. Truthfully, I couldn't imagine doing anything or being anywhere else.

As much as I appreciate getting nostalgic over your little trip down memory lane, could we get back to the problem of this doomsday bell? I get a facial tic every time this thing rings.

"Heidi could be right, Leo," I pointed out, walking back around the counter and hoisting myself up on the stool. "Technically, nothing bad has happened since we've come into possession of those wayward occult items."

I accidentally set off the small animated pumpkin that I'd set out on the counter. The lights inside the little porcelain decoration flickered on and off while playing a spooky tune. There were quite a few of these seasonal figurines strategically placed around the shop. As for the exterior, I'd used cornstalks, pumpkins, and had even strung a few rubber vampire bats from the awning to complete the ambiance.

"What if we're stressing ourselves out for nothing?" I asked, eyeing the candy corn in a dish that a skeleton held in his hand on the opposite side of the counter. Was the sugary treat any different than eating a donut first thing in the morning? I'm sure it had the same amount of calories. "We know for a fact that sometimes spirits have unfinished business here on our side of the veil. Maybe whatever they're dealing with is private, and they don't want us to intervene on their behalf."

First, could we please stop using the P word in connection with the evil objects you felt compelled to retrieve from the antique shop? You won't be so nonchalant about saying it when a spirit inhabits your body. Wait. Maybe you would. You wouldn't technically be you, would you? The new you would say anything to keep the old you at bay. You know what I mean? That's a lot of yous to keep up with. I've lost track of who's who, and now I've just confused myself.

Leo's ability to bewilder himself had a tad bit to do with those consequences I'd mentioned about the necromancy spell. He'd come out the other end of the incantation with a short-term memory loss issue. In full disclosure, it had affected his memory in general. It was as if Leo's brain activity had an intermittent short-circuit that went haywire every now and then.

Dark magic was nothing to sneeze at, and I stayed as far away from it as possible with good reason.

I'll have you know that I lost a pound. Technically, it was three-quarters of a pound, but it still counts if you round up.

Leo's appearance had also been affected by the spell, and by that I do mean quite drastically. His tail resembled a modern art masterpiece, his whiskers were pointed in odd directions all at once, tufts of black and orange hair stuck out every which away, and his left eye bulged out more than his right when he got excited. He looked so different from his previous self who had been my grandmother's companion that the residents of the town assumed he was a rescue cat I'd found in some shelter on my way to town. We didn't bother to correct them.

"Exactly, you guys. You both are worrying over nothing," Heidi concurred, carefully putting the lid on her travel mug. We'd been best friends practically our entire lives, so I had been beyond thrilled when she'd decided to follow me here and set up residence in Paramour Bay as the town's new accountant. She also knew my secret, which made it easier to carry on a side conversation with Leo when she was present. "Tomorrow is Halloween. Not only are we going to celebrate the holiday with the town square's trick or treating event, we're ringing in your birthday with a costume party at the pub afterward. We've been murder and mystery free for nearly two months. As much as I love all the supernatural excitement, we can last another week or two living mundane yet carefree lives of the uninitiated."

Oh, I don't think I mentioned that Leo and I had managed to get ourselves involved in numerous investigations over the past year. We'd solved a few murder mysteries, a kidnapping, an arson investigation, and even the case of an empty crypt with the help of my newfound talents. Residents of the afterlife had even dubbed us amateur sleuths in good standing. It was a plus that I dated the sheriff of Paramour Bay, who by the way only recently learned of my secret.

You're not the most orthodox witch on the planet, are you? And to set the record straight, my appearance is quite striking to those who bother to use a discerning eye…at least according to GQ Magazine.

Technically, witches telling humans about our existence went against coven rules. So were a lot of other things I might or might not have done in the last year. Anyway, we took it upon ourselves to help ensure the safety of the town's residents. Why wouldn't we? We had the ability to protect those close to us, especially when it came to an impending supernatural disaster. I'd say the ringing of a cesaral spirit bell fell into that category.

Agreed. Skippy and his mates rate pretty high on the doomsday scale, but a cesaral spirit bell takes the catnip.

"Earth to Raven," Heidi said with a laugh, though she may have repeated herself. I'd zoned out thinking about the bell's significance. "No more talk of cesaral spirit bells, occult items, or anything to do with the supernatural. Right now, you are Raven Lattice Marigold who owns a tea shop and celebrates her thirty-first birthday tomorrow with the man of her dreams. Speaking of the handsome sheriff, where is he this morning?"

I was going to take a page out of Heidi's book and not the family grimoire. Spells, enchantments, and incantations could definitely wait a couple of days. Starting now, all the doomsday predictions that Leo kept spouting were being placed on the back burner along with the real significance of Samhain. Samhain was the Celtic pagan festival we now recognized as All Hallows' Eve.

A few days off?

"Liam is getting things ready for the town's trick or treating event," I replied, matching her smile. Sheriff Liam Drake was not only attractive, kind, loyal and intelligent...he accepted me for what and who I am. He was everything I wanted wrapped up in a very big red bow. "I even got him to agree to wear a costume."

I could do with a few days off, provided I had the appropriate amount of catnip.

"Let me guess." Heidi held up a hand, fortifying herself with a sip of her coffee while Leo continued to ramble on about a mini-staycation. Her blue eyes sparkled with merriment, because she'd had the same problem with the man she was dating when it came to costumes. Neither Liam nor Detective Jack Swanson was the type of man to partake in dress-up games. "Liam has decided to go…as a sheriff."

You've convinced me, Raven. I'm now reevaluating my thoughts on this entire cesaral spirit bell thing. It would certainly put me out of my misery from listening to the two of you carry on about the men in your life. A few days of messing with Skippy and his ninja bandits are just what I need to get back on the right track.

"Maybe we need to find you a sleek, magnificent feline who can handle your mood swings," I countered, not in the least bit surprised when Leo jumped gracelessly from the counter with what sounded like a hiss of disapproval. His time of staring at the bell in question had come to an abrupt end. No doubt, he was going to curl up on his bed in the display window and take a nap. It was way too early for Leo to go traipsing around town. "Oh, come on. Would it be so bad for us to find you a friendly soulmate? You know, I heard Mindy rescued a tabby from a shelter last month."

"I heard that, too," Heidi piped in, eyeing Leo as if he were her next project. "Her name is Cupcake. I'm a great matchmaker, Leo."

That alone is enough to make me stay far away from Mindy and her new dessert dish. Besides, Heidi is my soulmate. We just need to figure out how to turn her into a sleek feline who has a thing for handsome tomcats such as myself.

"Oh, you should also know that I didn't want you to feel left out tomorrow," Heidi exclaimed, causing Leo to trip over his two front paws. "Do you like unicorns?"

Heidi slung her purse over her shoulder, adjusting the pink and grey scarf she'd expertly tied around her neck. Her sense of fashion was bar none, and she even wore a coordinating lipstick color to complete her ensemble. You can take the girl out of the city, but you can't take the city out of the girl. Right now, I'm pretty sure Leo was rethinking his crush on Heidi. He'd come to a complete stop the moment she'd dropped that brick by hinting at a unicorn costume.

Oh, this would successfully take my mind off the cesaral spirit bell. I was definitely taking pictures of Leo dressed for Halloween. I might even have to start a scrapbook.

That works both ways, Raven. Both ways. You can tell Heidi right now that there is no way in Hades that I'm dressing up as a freaking unicorn for Halloween. Nope. Not gonna happen.

"Leo, the baby pink and light blue horn even has glittery ribbons that stream down either side," Heidi said with excitement. She winked playfully at me, knowing full well she'd have to wrestle Leo to the ground in order to get the elastic band around his head. I'd actually pay to see that. "You're going to look fantastic. Trust me."

The bell above the tea shop's door chimed before Leo could respond to Heidi. I wasn't sure who jumped higher—me or Leo. Anything that sounded like a bell ringing recently seemed to spike our adrenaline in under a second. This instance was no different, and it was a wonder I hadn't choked on my favorite beverage. As it stood, I was going to have to get some paper towels to wipe off my hand where my coffee had sloshed all over the place.

Sweet angel of mercy, I think my nerves are frayed like they've been shredded with a cheese grater. Do cats get tachycardia? Is that a thing? We might need to call Dr. Jameson.

"Good morning, dear hearts," Elsie called out, still holding the door for Wilma. The two women were in their seventies and usually only came into the store on Monday morning, after their standing hair appointments. They really liked their scheduled routine, so something must be amiss to have them out and about on a Wednesday morning. "Raven, could you grab Wilma some chamomile tea? She needs something a bit calming after last night."

The old biddy might be onto something, Raven. Can you spike mine with some of my premium organic catnip? I need a little something to take the edge off. Preferably something that makes me fall into a coma for the next forty-eight hours to avoid the nightmare that I'm bound to have fighting off Heidi. I wonder if I can bribe Skippy to pretend to be me for a day. That would solve all my problems.

"What happened, Wilma?" I asked, sharing a concerned look with Heidi.

"It's more like what didn't happen," Elsie exclaimed, shuffling her way over to the tea leaf section. She squinted as she read the labels. "Wilma has recently taken to seeing things that aren't there, and I think it's because she drank a cup of that dandelion tea Pearl gave her as a birthday present last week."

Great. You're going to have all the elderly patrons hyped up on caffeine in this town. As if we didn't have enough problems as it is.

Well, there *was* quite a bit of caffeine in that type of tea blend. Having said that, there wasn't nearly enough to cause hallucinations. Pearl Saffron hadn't been able to get enough of the tea blend, and she'd been suggesting it to all her friends. She claimed it put a skip in her step.

Speaking of Skippy, I think I'm going to skip on out of here, Raven. All this commotion around All Hallows' Eve is probably what's got those spirits all riled up. I don't want to be around when that bell rings in the next doomsday.

I hopped off my stool and took the paper towel that Heidi had all but shoved in my hand. Wiping the excess coffee from my fingers, I made my way over to where Wilma was fiddling with a button on her jacket.

"Wilma, what happened last night?" I asked gently, wondering if there was some enchanting tea blend I could whip up in the back that might help Wilma with her hallucinations. It could have simply been a side effect of mixing her daily medications or maybe not getting enough sleep. Nan had a holistic remedy in the back room for such a problem. "Maybe I can help."

Wilma shot Elsie an irritated glance while motioning for me to come closer. Once our faces were two inches apart, she finally confessed what had taken place last night. Considering she'd done so in the faintest of whispers, I'm pretty sure I'd heard incorrectly.

"Could you repeat that?" I asked after clearing my throat. Please, please convince me that I'd heard wrong. I couldn't even bring myself to look at Leo, whose left eye was undoubtedly bulging while one of his crooked whiskers ticked back and forth uncontrollably. "I think I misunderstood. It's probably because I haven't had enough coffee myself."

"I saw my dead husband, Raven." Wilma gave up the pretense of whispering, apparently not caring anymore that her best friend thought she was losing her marbles. "Elsie doesn't believe me, but I'm telling you…Merle was standing right in the middle of our living room, handsome as could be and even wearing his favorite golfing hat I always hated. I buried it with him, you know."

There's a simple explanation to this, Raven. I'm not quite sure what that is, but you're going to figure it out without causing us any more problems. I'm ready. Right this second, Raven. Explain away. I'm waiting.

"Maybe an overload of caffeine wasn't the best idea to have so late at night," I said cautiously, grabbing onto Elsie's theory. There could very well be substance to such an excuse. "Right, Heidi?"

I should have known better than to ask Heidi her opinion on such matters. As much as Heidi might have wanted Leo and me not to focus on the bell, she absolutely loved the excitement provided by these side mysteries we always seemed to find ourselves involved in. Maybe it had something to do with the fact that she dealt with numbers all day. It had to be boring. I honestly didn't know, but she quickly stepped forward and joined us before I could distract her from asking any more questions.

"Did Merle talk to you?" Heidi asked, her blue eyes sparkling with interest. "Could you see through him? Tell me all about it."

Sweet angel of mercy, my beloved Heidi is going to be the death of me. You know, I've heard that about platonic love. It makes one reckless. I want you to know that if she ends up sending me to the afterlife, you're all coming with me.

Chapter Two

"**I**'VE GOT TO get to the office," Heidi said reluctantly after glancing at her watch. "Monty wanted to go over the fiscal numbers for the hardware store before the end of the year."

Heidi and Wilma had spent the last twenty minutes talking about her encounter with her dead husband. Leo hadn't moved from his spot near the coffee station, not having quite made it to his pillow in the display window where he normally perched. He was still giving Heidi a lethal sideways glare. He technically hadn't even moved a muscle since Heidi had encouraged Wilma to share details about her ghost encounter, with the exception of his recurrent facial tic—a bent whisker still twitching every now and then.

I was ringing up Elsie's order of chamomile tea, which she was purchasing for Wilma in her time of need. The two older ladies were practically inseparable, best friends forever, and I could just imagine how worried Elsie was about her companion.

You've given me hope, Raven.

"Call me later?" I asked Heidi pointedly, wanting to lecture her about opening up another spiritual can of worms.

My ability to do magic was getting better and better with each passing day, but former dead husbands coming back from the dead? Not so much. I avoided necromancy and everything connected to it, with the one exception being Leo.

I can breathe a little bit easier now. It's very commonplace for elderly humans to become senile and hallucinate toward the end, you know. This is a simple case of the lights being on, but no one is really home. Be nice to the old lady, Raven. I'm sure your time will come soon enough when you're nothing but a couple of sandwiches short of a picnic.

"Isn't she just darling?" Wilma came to stand next to Elsie at the counter, bumping elbows. "I bet Raven would believe her friend if she said she saw her dead husband. I mean, if she ever has one."

Ouch. Good thing my beloved Heidi didn't hear that slight dig about her social life.

I agreed with Leo, especially since Heidi's relationship with Detective Jack Swanson was in a wonderful place right now. Heidi and Jack had basically been dating for as long as Liam and I have, and I'd never been happier.

"You had too much caffeine before bedtime, Wilma." Elsie handed over a twenty-dollar bill with a sniff. "Merle has been long dead for well over a decade now. It's not like he suddenly got up and crawled out of his plot at the cemetery to come visit you."

"I agree," Wilma replied, causing Elsie to nod in approval. Her frown deepened when Wilma continued with her train of thought. "It was my Merle's spirit from the other side. His body is long gone by now. He must have something to tell me, maybe something I missed after he passed over. I've watched television shows about these types of occurrences on the Discovery Channel. They're quite real, you know. Come to think of it, the show might have aired on the Travel Channel. I'm not sure, but maybe I should give them a call and see who can look into things like this. They can send out one of their paranormal teams to find out what unfinished business Merle has here. He always did buy those lottery tickets. Maybe he left behind a safe deposit box I don't know about."

Elsie actually seemed to be considering Wilma's explanation, while Leo and I could only stare at them in horror. This situation was getting out of hand. Had I been one hundred percent sure that Merle hadn't visited Wilma, I'm positive I would have had a good laugh over the antics of these two best friends.

Busybodies. That's what they are, and it's your job to set them on the straight and narrow path, Raven. Fix this before our quaint little coastal town is overrun by camera crews and overzealous paranormal investigators who might just stumble upon something that could end up outing us on national television. Oh, I feel an asthma attack coming on. Where are my edibles?

"I never thought about that, Wilma." Elsie held out her weathered hand for her change. "Did you ever check the tickets that Merle bought right before his heart attack? Maybe that is why he collapsed."

"I never could bring myself to open his wallet," Wilma said, sneaking a candy corn from the dish. She chewed it slowly before opting to take another one. "It still sits on top of our dresser, rest his soul."

"You really need to get over that type of sentimentality, Wilma." Elsie was the more practical of the two, so it didn't surprise me that she was ready to cash in on some theoretical winning lottery ticket. "We could take a lot of cruises with that type of money, not that we don't have enough already."

Is there a reason you're not fixing this dreadful calamity? Now is not the time to hesitate, Raven.

"I think a lottery ticket purchased that many years ago would have expired," I said as gently as I could, given the circumstances. Wilma clearly still loved her husband, but it was very doubtful that he'd visited her about a lottery ticket. There was one way to find out, though. "Um, Merle wasn't still hanging around at the house when you left this morning, was he?"

I hadn't realized that Leo had finally made his way to his bed in the display window, but his loud gasp of horror resounded in my ears.

Why would you ask such a thing? Take it back, Raven. Right now, because I don't have enough edibles stashed away to handle this kind of delusional behavior...on their part or yours.

Even Elsie blinked a few times, as if it hadn't occurred to her that Merle still might be lingering around the house. Depending on the answer, I might actually have a way of making them pull back on their ghost-believing reins.

"Well, no," Wilma replied with confusion. She pointed the candy corn she held in between her shaking fingers my way. "Merle stayed for a bit, but when I looked again after calling Elsie...well, he'd simply disappeared."

"There you have it," Elsie exclaimed, snatching up the tea blend I'd put into one of the shop's logo-stamped bags. "You never should have believed Pearl when she said that the dandelion tea blend gave her a boost of energy. She always overstates things. Don't you remember when she had you try that face cream she discovered in that stylish New York beauty parlor? You lost both your eyebrows, and now you have to draw them on your face."

Well, that explains a lot. I thought good ol' Wilma had gone to clown school back in her day. Remind me to stay far away from Purple Pearl's recommended beauty regiment.

Pearl had thought she was going for a shade of silver, but she had more of a purple sheen to her hair now. Cindy, the only professional hair stylist in town, had tried to rectify the problem. Unfortunately, Pearl was a bit colorblind and was completely in love with the results of the dye job.

"Don't you worry none," Elsie reassured Wilma with a pat on the shoulder. "Tonight, you'll drink the chamomile tea and fall right to sleep. You have a good day, Raven."

Wilma momentarily snuck back to get a few more candy corns, appearing a bit more relieved now that she was considering that her husband's ghost was nothing more than a side effect from overindulging in too much late-night caffeine.

Was it possible?

Could Elsie be right about the dandelion tea blend?

Anything is possible. Now that the dead husband turned ghost crisis is over, I'm going to finish my edibles and take a much-deserved nap before I go searching for Skippy and his band of ninja misfits. You're on bell duty. Don't let it ring. It's all up to you now.

I rolled my eyes as I tossed the soiled paper towels I'd used to clean up the coffee into the small wastebasket behind me. More coffee was needed stat. Grabbing my cup, I walked around the counter toward the shop's coffee station.

"It's not like I have control over the spirits, Leo," I said, carefully pumping the lever on top of the carafe with the exact amount of pressure so that I wouldn't spill a drop of coffee. "Ted spoke with Ivan when we first heard the bell ring. Nothing unusual happened at the cemetery back then, but maybe it wouldn't hurt to have Ted ask again at tonight's poker game."

Ted was actually a wax golem made in the form of TV's Lurch from *The Addams Family*. Seriously, we have a wax museum at the entrance to our small town. Anyway, he had the signature whitish blond hair, somewhat square features, quite a few chipped teeth, and stood about six and a half foot tall. Nan had wanted someone to keep her company and help with gathering material components for spells, so she'd cast a series of animation object incantations to bring him to life. He currently lived at the back of my inherited property in a small house.

Shed, Raven. It's a shed. A Ted-Shed. The Crayola actually lives in a box.

Okay, it might be a shed, but I'm pretty sure the interior was magically sublime. I mean, Ted was able to get his hands on the rarest ingredients that naturally came from faraway locales. It's not like he had Leo's ability to become invisible and teleport himself to faraway places other people couldn't drive to on a daily basis.

Anyway, Ted attended a standing weekly poker game with the groundskeeper at the cemetery. We previously had no idea that the older gentleman's body had been inhabited by a grim reaper. Don't worry. Apparently, the real Ivan had crossed over to the afterlife long ago and our friendly neighborhood reaper was just making use of his physical body. With that said, Ted and Ivan were buddies who played poker every Wednesday night, much to Leo's chagrin.

Go ahead. Rub it in my face that I'm not invited to join the only local supernatural poker game hosted by a grim reaper. My day just keeps getting better and better.

"We didn't realize it then, but Ivan is allergic to cats," I gently reminded Leo as I sprinkled a bit of cinnamon in my coffee. Not wanting this cup to go to waste with my clumsiness, I chose one of the proper-sized lids and secured it firmly to the rim. "Not the actual grim reaper, but the body he has borrowed. I wonder if allergy medicine would work on a dead body that's been reanimated to serve the reaper's purposes."

You just have a special knack for inducing headaches, don't you?

"I'm trying to rationalize for you here, in case you didn't notice."

Instead of walking back around the counter to sit on the stool, I crossed the floor closer to Leo so that I could get a better look out the display window. I couldn't prevent the smile that crossed my lips when I spotted Liam talking with Eugene. The older gentleman was best friends with Albert. The two of them played chess in front of Monty's hardware store every afternoon.

Wake me up around noon. I should have enough energy by then to go searching for Skippy's hibernation hideout. Those ninja squirrels always steer me away from a certain acorn tree, but I'm onto them this year. I'll rain destruction upon their squirrelly plans.

Trust me, Skippy and his friends had nothing to worry about concerning their upcoming hibernation season. Leo wasn't capable of climbing high distances due to his weight, and Skippy was smart enough to make sure his hideout was well out of reach.

My smile did begin to fade when I noticed Liam put his hand on Eugene's shoulder in reassurance about something that must have been bothering the older gentleman. Once the conversation was finished, Eugene slowly made his way to the diner where he had breakfast with Albert every morning. The two friends were inseparable, much like Elsie and Wilma.

Had something happened with Eugene that the gossip queens hadn't gotten around to knowing about? Or had Elsie and Wilma been too distracted with Merle's ghostly sighting to inform me of the town's latest chinwag?

The palm of my right hand began to heat up just a tad, warning me that not all was as it seemed. I cautiously looked over my shoulder to where the cesaral spirit bell sat next to the cash register. It remained silent, but ominously so.

You're making it very hard for me to get some shuteye, Raven. In case you've forgotten, you're holding a cup of hot coffee. Now, go away and do some inventory or something equally stimulating.

Leo settled deeper into his cat bed that I had strategically set inside the display window so that he could take advantage of the sun's rays. The day was a bit overcast, but that wouldn't stop Leo from catching some well-deserved zzzs.

Was Leo right? Had the sudden warmth in the palm of my hand come from my coffee cup? I opened and closed my fingers, hoping the heat would dissipate now that I only held the cup in my left hand.

You see, I utilized energy from the earth to cast spells. The elements surrounding me made it possible to generate magical incantations. I also had the ability to perceive when danger or a threat was near me by unconsciously harnessing the energy in the palm of my hand as a defense mechanism. Granted, I was still getting used to understanding exactly how my abilities worked, but I was slowly getting there.

You tossed an energy ball at a bumblebee last month. I'm pretty sure he wasn't presenting any real danger to your life, which tells me that you still have quite a lot to work on in the witchcraft department.

"Hey, the little stinker was dive bombing me," I said defensively, remembering that day like it was yesterday. I'd started swinging my arms a million miles an hour. Unfortunately, I'd inadvertently sent an energy ball hurtling through the air. Thankfully, the bumblebee was very good at avoiding threats to its existence. "Besides, that bumblebee was very good at ducking in midair. He was fine, though I do wonder if he's planning his revenge with another ambush."

Leo adjusted himself on his pillow, rolling himself onto his back with his munchkin legs sticking straight up toward the ceiling. It wasn't until he fell asleep that the light snoring began and his tongue slipped out to dangle from the side of his mouth. He was the very picture of relaxation.

I left him to sleep, elated when I saw Liam looking both ways before crossing the street. When I'd first moved to Paramour Bay, he'd figured out quickly that I preferred coffee over tea. He even used to sneak me coffee from the diner on a daily basis. Now that I had the coffee station inside the tea shop, he'd gotten into the habit of stopping in every morning before taking a drive through the residential areas of our small town to check on the older residents.

"Morning, beautiful," Liam said after coming through the entrance with a charming smile on his handsome features. He'd gotten a haircut yesterday, but Cindy had left it long enough on top to where his natural waves could still be seen. "You know, I just had the oddest conversation with Eugene."

Once again, the palm of my hand began to tingle as I lifted myself up on my tiptoes to greet him with a kiss. Given the time of year, I was ecstatic that I could wear my favorite pair of knee-high boots. The small heel didn't get me close to Liam's six foot height, but he leaned down to make reaching his lips a bit of an easier task.

"I saw the two of you talking across the street." We walked side by side to the coffee station, while I was running theories through my mind as to what topics might have been covered in that brief conversation. "Is everything okay? Does this have something to do with Albert? I didn't see him over there with Eugene."

Liam began to pump the top of the carafe and pour himself a

cup of black coffee. His brows were furrowed a bit, another hint that the coffee in my hand had nothing to do with the heat in my palm. Just when my attention landed on the cesaral spirit bell next to the cash register, Liam's did as well. I was really happy that I could hear Leo's light snores drifting from the display window.

"Out of curiosity, has the bell rung recently?"

I blinked, wishing I could do the same with my hearing. Liam really hadn't just asked me that question, had he? If he had, that would mean…

"Please tell me that Eugene hasn't seen a ghost lately," I whispered, setting my own cup on the table. I was afraid I'd collapse the paper sides with my grip. Liam's hand was quite a bit sturdier, so I grabbed ahold of his forearm in desperation. "Just say the *no* word, and we can have a normal day with me selling tea and you keeping the town safe from jaywalkers."

Telling Liam about my family lineage had been the best decision I'd ever made, besides uprooting my life from New York City to Paramour Bay. He'd handled it as well as could be expected, and he'd been beyond supportive of my continued training that Leo and I still took time out of our day to complete.

"It could be nothing," Liam hedged, rocking back on the heels of his work boots. He was wearing his brown leather bomber jacket now that the weather had finally changed to match the season. Today's high was only going to be fifty-nine degrees, which was fine by me. I had an obsession with not only boots but also turtlenecks. "Eugene was walking past the station when I was exiting, and I noticed him chuckling underneath his breath. I asked why, and he said that he could have sworn he saw his brother crossing the street. When Eugene did a double take, no one was there. Then he went on and on about how turning senile during his old age was going to be a riot for the town's gossip mill. Now, I'm chalking this up to exactly that, Raven. Right? Please tell me that Eugene seeing his brother has to do with old age and the loss of a few brain cells along the way."

Liam sounded a lot like Leo in this moment, but he might take offense to the comparison. Not that he didn't like Leo. Quite the contrary. Once Leo had gotten over me telling Liam the truth about my lineage, he'd come to accept my relationship with Liam. But Leo tended to be a bit dramatic over such things, and my sweet sheriff might take it as a slight that I thought he was doing the same.

Only neither one of them were wrong this time around.

Two ghost sightings in the last twelve hours or so?

That was definitely cause for concern if they were actual sightings.

Liam and Leo wanted so badly for me to tell them that the sighting of two separate ghosts were just a figment of two elderly people's imagination. Unfortunately, I wasn't so sure that was the case anymore.

I'm going to need to eat another edible, aren't I?

Chapter Three

"**T**ED."

I'd poked my head out the glass door of the tea shop not five seconds after Ted had walked past the shop window on his way to visit Mindy's boutique shop. Long story short, my wax golem helper had fallen in love with a mannequin. Seriously, he came to visit her nearly every single day the store was open for patrons. The residents of the town just assumed Ted was extraordinarily unique in some fashion or another. They had no idea he was supernatural and found a natural affection for an inanimate object that was a wonderful listener and equally attractive...not that Ted had much to say.

"Ted, I need your help once you've said your good mornings," I whispered, catching sight Cora Barnes walking toward us. She wasn't my favorite fan, having what one might call a difficult relationship with my mother. I called it a very convoluted feud. Cora and her husband owned the malt shop that was located in between my tea shop and Mindy's boutique. The last thing I wanted was to get into a long, drawn-out conversation with Mrs. Barnes about anything. "Could you come inside when you're done, please?"

This is a bad idea. Have you considered that Eugene really is a few acorns shy of a full sapling? Speaking of acorns, this bell situation is keeping me from my preordained destiny—the annihila-

tion of Skippy and his band of ninja squirrels.

I ducked back inside before glancing across the street. Liam had stayed with me a bit, talking over the two separate reports of townsfolk having seen the spirits of loved ones long since passed. There was still a chance that this could all be chalked up to coincidence or mass hysteria.

You remind me of a long-necked ostrich who likes to put his head in the sand while describing how wonderful the weather is at the moment. Ignoring an uncomfortable situation won't make it go away. Trust me, I've tried it a lot during our spell casting lessons.

"I could accept that we might have a spirit invasion if someone younger than seventy declared they had experienced a ghost sighting," I replied, compromising my position on the subject. "When you think about it, Wilma isn't used to ingesting that much caffeine, especially right before bedtime. As for Eugene, he was crossing the intersection and could have easily been thinking about his brother. The image he'd caught in his peripheral vision might not have been anything more than a trick of the light or a shadow he thought was something else."

In case you hadn't noticed, it's overcast. Your shadow theory is a few sunbeams shy of likely.

"Then maybe it was a cornstalk caught in the wind," I suggested, finally catching sight of Ted slowly strolling past the display window. He was very methodical in everything he did, and that included walking. "I mean, there are cornstalks attached to every lamppost. It's plausible that one might have blown away."

Are you telling me that Eugene mistook a cornstalk for his dead breather? Maybe you need another cup of coffee. I'd offer you some of my edibles, but I'm rationing my supply until Beetle comes into work tomorrow morning. You never know what harebrained idea someone might come up with before I can resupply.

One, I just happened to know that Leo practically had an unlimited supply of vacuum-packed catnip edibles stuffed away in a bugout bag he kept on the shelf next to the shop's rarely used rear entrance. Two, the mere mention of Beetle had me wondering about the wisdom of this entire scenario and imagining reasons we shouldn't do the unthinkable.

You are absolutely not doing the unthinkable. That's the reason it's called the unthinkable. Try not to think about it. You march yourself right on over to that coffee station and pour yourself another cup and take a chill pill. After you've consumed copious amounts of your sanity saver, you'll see the error of contemplating the unthinkable.

"You're right." The last time we'd involved my mother, she'd literally caused lightning to strike my cottage. "It's best to utilize that option as our last resort. We'll call that the failsafe option."

For a brief moment, I wasn't even sure that coffee could bring you back from the ledge. That was my failsafe.

Beetle was the previous town accountant who had sold his accounting firm to Heidi. He'd all but hired himself on as my part-time employee to keep himself busy in retirement. In summation, Beetle had fallen head over heels in love with my mother years ago when she'd attended high school here. She'd renewed his interest subsequent to my return. Let's just say that the two of them are polar opposites, like fire and ice. I was wondering when they'd implode.

You have such a tendency to understate things, Raven. They are more like a stick of dynamite and a kitchen match. The fallout could rain down for years to come.

I was pacing back and forth in between the high-top tables when Ted finally walked into the shop, while Leo had decided a nap wasn't going to be anywhere in his near future. He was currently back on the counter, his bulging left eye focused suspiciously on the cesaral spirit bell.

"Is everything alright, Ms. Raven?"

I've already gone into depth about Ted's appearance, but I should also mention his quirky personality. He was beyond loyal, super kind, and—

My least favorite Crayola color?

I shot Leo a glare over my shoulder, grateful that Ted couldn't hear Leo's commentary. Only witches, warlocks, and other familiars could hear him drone on.

I was going to say Ted is concise. His oral communication skills tended to be very brief and to the point. When I'd first met him, I'd thought his sentences were kind of choppy. The more I got to know him, the more I realized he just didn't mince words. He simply said what needed to be said and nothing more.

"Ted, do you remember when I needed you to ask Ivan about the sudden appearance of roaming spirits?" I inquired, rubbing the palm of my right hand. There was still a bit of leftover tingling sensations from when I'd seen Liam speaking with Eugene. "I need you to ask him again."

"Has something transpired?" Ted asked, his straight eyebrows making a perfect V in concern.

"Well, that depends," I replied warily, still hoping that the two sightings were nothing to get worry about. "Wilma and Eugene both claim to have seen the spirits of their dearly departed loved ones recently."

Dead people. You can say it, Raven. They saw dead people. I'm pretty sure there was a movie made about a boy who could see and talk to dead people. It was very scary stuff that I'd rather not personally experience. Been there, done that, got the t-shirt.

Technically, Leo was right. We'd already encountered the spirit of an older witch when she'd had some unfinished business in the human world. We'd helped escort her familiar back through the veil. As a thank you, the fairy had left Leo with a glittery lipstick kiss that had stained the fur on his front right paw.

Don't remind me. I still can't get this annoying glitter off my fur. Do you see why the ringing of this bell is unacceptable? A cat can only explain so much glitter.

"What is Mr. Leo saying?"

I knew there was a redeeming quality in that lump of wax.

"Leo is just concerned about the sightings, plus the fact that the bell has rung a total of five times since we've discovered its existence at the antique shop. I guess we're wondering if those two sightings were only two of the five rings we heard. It's possible more sightings were made and not reported."

Ted rubbed his large hands down the lapel of his black suit in contemplation. He only wore suits cut in the style of the late 1800s with paisley handkerchiefs folded perfectly in the outer pocket. With that said, his whitish-blond hair always stuck up a bit in the back to make him seem more human.

"I will speak with Ivan this evening, Ms. Raven."

I waited for the relief to pour over me at Ted's acquiesce, but the respite never came.

"Maybe I can come with you," I offered, hoping that speaking to Ivan in person would alleviate my concern. "I've never met Ivan. Maybe it's time we were introduced."

"Mr. Ivan isn't very social, for obvious reasons." Ted warned, clearly not liking my suggestion. He shifted uncomfortably on his polished dress shoes.

One would think a grim reaper would need to be social, but

maybe Ivan remained silent as he escorted souls into the afterlife. *That isn't depressing or anything. Listen, I say we crash the poker game tonight. You can speak with Ivan, cast a spell to get rid of his cat allergies, and then you can leave me to win everyone's cash. By the way, ask Crayola Head what the stakes are for tonight. I should be prepared.*

"Please, Ted? Maybe if I tell Ivan myself what has been happening around town, he'll have some insight for me." I wasn't beyond begging at this point. "I mean, what if there's some simple solution…like the veil between us and the afterlife being thin this time of year? After all, All Hallows' Eve is tomorrow."

Well, that rather odd theory came out of left field.

"I should probably ask Ivan first," Ted offered, his frown still in place.

Let me guess. The grim reaper doesn't like surprises. Hey, do you think he harbors resentment about me not crossing over with Rosemary? I never thought about it, but maybe he has some type of appointment ledger with everyone's scheduled death date.

"That's just morbid," I muttered, gathering my long, black hair and bringing it around my left shoulder. "Ted, do you think you could ask Ivan about it this afternoon? Leo and I can accompany you this evening if Ivan gives us his permission."

I wasn't sure what would happen if we managed to upset the grim reaper, but I didn't want to find out.

That's probably the smartest thing you said all morning. Surprising Death shouldn't antagonize him at all.

"I will pay another visit to my beloved first," Ted said, finally relenting and causing me to breathe a little easier.

"Perfect." I stepped forward and gave Ted an impromptu hug. He never knew what to do in these circumstances. He slow-patted my back awkwardly until I released his thin waist. "Thank you, Ted. Leo mentioned saving my sanity, but this is what will do the trick. I just want to make sure we aren't going to have a spirit invasion of the entire town for Halloween."

"I understand, Ms. Raven."

Ted exited the tea shop, making a hard, left turn on the sidewalk in order to stroll down to Mindy's boutique.

There is a bright spot to this predicament, if you think about it.

"Leo, you're still staring at that bell as if it's going to grow legs and walk to the cemetery itself," I said wryly as I made my way over to the coffee station. Maybe I'd even add an espresso shot this time for additional courage in light of what we could be facing later this evening. "The only bright spot I'm seeing is that neither spirit that we know of decided to hang around for more than a mere glimpse."

I'm just saying that this is the perfect time of year for a dilemma such as this. The spirits can walk amongst the other people dressed up in their costumes, and they would be none the wiser.

I shot Leo a contemplative glance, attempting to figure out what his game plan was in this situation. He was usually all doom and gloom, and here he was being an optimist.

"What gives?" I asked, refusing to have the wool pulled over my eyes.

Oh, that.

"Yes, that," I stated, dumping the espresso shot into my cup of coffee. It was going to be a long day until Ted returned with news of our meeting with the grim reaper tonight. It wasn't like such an event was an everyday occurrence. "What are you up to?"

Fine. If you must know, I'm tapping out for the remainder of the day.

"You are not tapping out of this mystery, Leo." There were

things that needed to be done, such as Leo popping in to visit Wilma or Eugene to make sure they weren't talking to their long-deceased loved ones. "We have work to do."

Ninja squirrel work, to be exact. I've been neglecting my duties, Raven. The squirrel apocalypse is just as important as a spirit apocalypse. Squirrels by day, spirits by night. That's my new motto.

"Leo, don't you dare—"

You're on bell duty, Raven. Accept your fate for whom the bell tolls.

And just like that, Leo disappeared from the counter, leaving a puff of orange and black fur floating in his wake. I should have just taken that espresso in a shot, especially after my fate had all but been sealed.

Yes.

By that, I meant that the cesaral spirit bell decided to ring once more.

"Leo, get your glitter-stained paw back here!"

Chapter Four

*I*WONDER WHO *would win—a small coastal town full of ninja squirrels or a half-dozen, soul-possessing supernatural spirits?*

Thankfully, Leo had materialized back inside the tea shop the minute I'd frantically demanded his presence. A few hours had passed with me making a few phone calls to Liam and Heidi, both of whom claimed they'd heard nothing else from any of the residents concerning spirit visits or odd sightings of any sort.

I'd put my stash of premium organic catnip on the ninja squirrels. Before you summoned me back here, I was able to get a peek at their acorn storage operation. I wasn't impressed. It seemed completely random to me. Skippy's minions were scattered all over town and had no logical plan for collecting those acorns for their extended winter hibernation. You know, I just realized how much Skippy and I have in common. My minions are operating totally outside the box, too.

"If you're comparing me to one of those ninja squirrels, you can stop right there, Mr. Doom and Gloom," I warned, pointing a pen in Leo's direction. We were both back at the counter in close proximity to the cesaral spirit bell. "I think I have a plan."

It better be improved from that idea you had earlier about calling your mother. My nerves are already frayed to the breaking point. I don't need the Wicked Witch of the East here to burn the entire town down. I'm not sure Beetle has nearly enough catnip in stock for me to be able to deal with your mother and her half-baked ideas right now.

"On the bright side, I don't think you'll be put into that position if this works out. The bell rang twice at the antique shop, twice at home, and twice here at the shop. Do you see the pattern?"

I have paws, you know. I can count, which is how I know that Beetle needs to place another order for my edibles. Once I vacuum seal enough of those puppies for emergency rations, I only have enough fresh ones on hand to get through the end of the week. Oh, by the way, there's a charge on your PayPal account for a live squirrel trap. Just ignore it. It's a business-related expenditure. Just tell Heidi that she needs to write it off on our taxes at the end of the year.

"You're missing the point," I said, enthusiasm setting in now that I'd unraveled part of the mystery. "The tone was decidedly different in each location the bell has rung, Leo."

Leo remained silent, as if waiting for me to enlighten him further. The only hint that he was taking my explanation seriously was the tic in one of his crooked whiskers.

"What if the bell notifies its owner of a spirit's presence, but does so by registering distance?"

I quickly looked over my shoulder at the clock hanging on the wall behind me. Lunch time had finally arrived, and I could close the shop for a half an hour while I tested out my somewhat farfetched theory. It was so much so that even I was suspicious of its viability. Seeing as I wasn't sure how many places I would have to test in order to obtain proof of my initial hypothesis, it was best I grab my coat and get started. Before I could walk into the back room, another bell chimed...this time, the one above the entrance to the shop.

I never thought I'd say this in all my nine lives, but I'm not perturbed in the least that our resident warlock is paying us a visit.

Leo was talking about Rye Dolgiram, the man who'd just entered the tea shop. I guess one could say that Rye was the adoptive son of my great Aunt Rowena, and therefore was one of my relatives. Truthfully, there was so much more that went with that story.

You see, Aunt Rowena was my grandmother's sister. The story goes that Nan had been excommunicated from the coven due to fraternizing with a human being rather than another supernatural like herself. That was a big no-no by coven rules, and it had put a wedge in their sibling relationship. Nan chose to move to Paramour Bay to begin a new life away from the coven, and Aunt Rowena chose to stay with what Nan saw as a superficial group of witches.

You might want to mention the budding war between the factions and the fact that your wicked witch auntie is leading the charge for the opposition. On second thought, getting out and seeing the sights with the doomsday bell in hand might be better than consorting with the progeny of the enemy.

"I'm not your enemy, Leo," Rye replied amusingly, pausing at one of the high-top tables for a sample of vanilla caramel tea that I'd added into this fall's inventory. "I just had an early lunch over at the diner and discovered something that should be very interesting to all of us."

Like the fact that you're consorting with a wicked witch who would happily turn you into a reptile with a simple blink of those long, creepy eyelashes? It's like she spelled two spiders to live on her face.

Leo shuddered in disgust while I tried not to take offense at Leo's description of Aunt Rowena, especially seeing as all the

Marigold women had basically the same features—long black hair, emerald green eyes, and high cheekbones. The only attribute that I could have done without were my hips. I personally liked my long eyelashes, but I did see why Leo would make that remark about Aunt Rowena and her tendency to overuse mascara. I'm pretty sure she used a triple coat of the thick black mess every morning.

"What did you find interesting?" I asked cautiously, knowing we had more important things to worry about than how much makeup Aunt Rowena wore on a daily basis.

I watched Rye very carefully for any sign that he wasn't telling me the entire truth. We'd come to an agreement of sorts, and he wasn't a bad warlock to have on my side if things went sideways.

You forget that he's from the dark side. They'll never turn us, Raven. Never. We're just like the Marines…Semper Fidelis!

As far as I knew, Rye was staying clear of the budding war himself. He was wary of the council for very different reasons than we were, and it had something to do with his ancestors. Aunt Rowena knew more about Rye's past than she was letting on, but he'd basically been living on the streets at a very young age when she'd *accidentally* come across him and snapped him up as her own.

If you believe that, I have a catnip farm in Alaska to sell you.

"I guess Elsie and Wilma were overheard talking about her run-in with Merle's spirit last night," Rye began, bringing his sample cup of tea over to the counter. His dark eyes drifted down to the bell, signifying that he knew exactly what it was used for in context of its creation. "Trixie was making her rounds, talking to the diners and such, when she mentioned having a *dream* about her best friend from high school paying her a visit."

The way Rye had stressed the word *dream* told me that he didn't believe for a second that Trixie's best friend had been a figment of her unconscious imagination.

"If you're here to find out if the cesaral spirit bell has rung...it already has," I admitted, coming right out with the truth. "Six times, to be exact."

And you wonder why I continually have to ingest catnip on an hourly basis. Sweet angel of mercy! Why on earth would you go and admit to something crazy like that? In case you forgot, he's got too many ties with more wicked witches besides your mother's aunt for us to be telling him all of our secrets.

"Leo, I'm not the bad guy you seem to think I am," Rye said, not appearing too concerned about Leo's accusations. "I'd previously seen an item at the antique store that I was interested in buying, but Lydia told me that you'd already purchased all of her occult items. It wasn't a stretch to put two and two together after hearing a few stories about the residents seeing their long-lost loved ones. If you want, I can talk to Ivan before the game tonight to see if there's anything unusual going on over at the cemetery."

I covered my face with my hands, knowing full well how Leo was going to react to Rye's claim of being invited to the weekly supernatural poker game.

I'm sorry, Mister Warlock. I think we misheard you. You said that you're going to the cemetery before the poker game in order to speak with the grim reaper, correct? It was almost as if you implied you were going to be playing in the game, which is where I'm sure we got our wires crossed.

Rye met my gaze and grimaced, having realized that he'd just lit the match to a powder keg of one very vengeful familiar. It was kind of humorous to watch him backtrack and try to save his skin from the ravages of numerous sharp claws.

"Don't Ted and Ivan play poker on Wednesday nights?" Rye asked, as if he were just finding out about such a weekly event. "That's tonight, right? Like I said, I'll just swing by the cemetery to pay them a little visit before the game."

"Ted is one step ahead of you," I added, not wanting there to be a break in the conversation. Leo's left eye was bulging, and a few other whiskers had joined in on the ticking party. "I actually want to speak with Ivan myself. Ted sometimes doesn't always get straight to the point, if you know what I mean."

"Well, I just stopped by to offer you help should you find that the veil has been pierced due to the proximity of All Hallows' Eve. We know just how thin it can be this time of year." Rye glanced over my shoulder at the large clock before finishing the rest of the vanilla caramel tea sample. "I've got to finish a job earlier than scheduled if I want to have dinner with Rowena."

You mean you'll be driving to Windsor this afternoon, thus confirming that you weren't invited to the weekly supernatural poker game, right?

Once again, Rye seemed to have walked himself right into another trap regarding that pesky card game and Rowena's whereabouts. Leo might actually be onto something though, because Windsor was over an hour away. Driving time, eating dinner, and then socializing a bit would definitely have Rye arriving back in town after the game had gotten well underway. Otherwise, that would mean…

Don't even think it, Raven. You'll put it out into the universe, and then it's all over but the toad spell.

"Are you saying that Aunt Rowena is in town?" I asked cautiously, unable to stop myself from asking the burning question Leo and I were both wondering. "As in here locally? In Paramour Bay?"

Leo let his weight drag his body down, all but plopping himself in defeat on the counter. I'm pretty sure his whiskers quivered when he blew a raspberry in exasperation at my determination in seeking an answer.

"Would you rather not know her location and just randomly bump into Aunt Rowena on the street?" I muttered, not caring that Rye could hear our conversation. He was practically raised by the woman. He knew full well what she was capable of when it came to getting what she wanted. "I'd rather be prepared."

I'd rather be in the park disrupting a squirrelpocalypse dooms-day plan, but you don't see me getting what I want today, now do you?

"Aunt Rowena is having some renovations done to her house this week, so she asked if she could stay with me for the duration," Rye replied, using the small wastebasket near the counter to throw away his sample cup. "I'm surprised she didn't stop by the tea shop today."

My mother had the capacity to arch an eyebrow in that im-peccable, irritating way I'd grown to admire. I did my best to mimic her. There was no way that Aunt Rowena was having renovations done on her house. She wouldn't trust anyone with that task except for Rye.

Really? That's the lie you sniffed out? Rowena doesn't simply stop by the tea shop to visit. That woman has never set foot in here to my knowledge, and I doubt that she'd ever make it across the threshold without eating some magic. I often wonder if my beloved Rosemary cast a warding spell over this sanctuary. Nothing like the present to find out.

"I'd go with Leo's pick, if I were you." Rye gave a light laugh, but there was sadness in his eyes that hit me directly in my heart. "You both know I never go near the coven. Rowena and I always meet somewhere in the middle when we want to spend time with one another. I would never risk working on her house, which is why I gave her some references on who to use for a kitchen remodel. She also wanted a specific octagonal room dedicated to casting magic."

I'm pretty sure this a foot in mouth example. I hope you feel good about yourself.

"Raven didn't mean anything by her assumption, Leo." Rye tapped the counter as he turned to leave. "You should know that the council is at a breaking point. Rowena is just trying to protect herself and those who have chosen her side to fight the bylaws."

By this time, Rye had reached the front door. The fact that he forgave me for being so insensitive was just another bout of guilt. I couldn't imagine being a teenager on the street with nowhere to call home, let alone one with unexplained powers. Then to be forced to live somewhere else, all because the coven wanted to know more about his abilities and where he came from. Aunt Rowena had done nothing but protect Rye, and here I was accusing her of ulterior motives when all she wanted done was some renovations on her house.

Just face facts. You're a horrible person, Raven. Always with the negative vibes.

"I'll leave the two of you to...well, to do your thing. I just wanted to offer my help with the cesaral spirit bell should you need it. After all, tomorrow is All Hallows' Eve." Rye lifted a hand to signal goodbye while using the other to open the door. "I'll talk to the two of you later."

You should check to see if I'm right about that warding spell. I sleep here, you know. I could die of a heart attack should I wake up from a sun nap to find that frightful face hovering over me.

"Rye said that Aunt Rowena was staying with him for a week. She hasn't stopped in yet, and she probably won't," I assured him, wondering if it was best to ignore the fact that Rowena was roaming about town. Surely, she'd be gone by the weekend. "I guess it's a good thing we bought all of the occult items from the antique shop. Who knows what Aunt Rowena would have done with that type of inventory. She—"

Leo began using his claws to quickly scramble back on the counter, cutting me off mid-sentence. In his panic mode, the candy dish came very close to sliding off the edge. I lunged and caught it from falling to the floor.

"What has gotten into you?" I asked, amazed that so many tufts of hair could stand on end in unison. His tail was so puffy that it was hard to tell the tip curled over like a closet hanger. "Leo?"

By this time, he was literally shaking his right paw and frantically licking the fairy mark. Oh, this wasn't good. I began to cautiously look around the tea shop for any sign of danger. I'd come to the conclusion a few months ago that the lipstick kiss was similar to the palm of my hand. The mark on Leo's fur seemed to sense when danger was near.

"Leo, are you—"

I don't know about you, but I could sure enjoy an edible treat right about now.

I watched in stunned silence as Leo calmly sat up straight, all of his fur returning to normal, licking his whiskers. It was as if nothing had happened. The adrenaline flowing through my veins began to slow down, along with my heartrate.

Another short-term memory loss at its best.

What are you talking about, Raven?

"Nothing," I murmured, knowing Leo's memories would return momentarily. At least I hoped so, because all this bell ringing combined with Aunt Rowena was enough to give any witch a spot of paranoia. "Listen, I was just going to close up the shop for a bit. I want to see if the cesaral spirit bell has different tones when rung in difference places."

You're going to ring the bell on purpose? The same one that tells us when spirits are near? Oh, wait. It's all coming back to me now. Not the Celine Dion song, but the last few moments.

"The bell has rung a total of six times now, Ted is seeing if we can speak with Ivan tonight about the veil between this life and the afterlife, and Aunt Rowena is lurking around town." I finally collected my light jacket from the back room, sliding my arms into the sleeves while Leo digested the main points of today's three-ring circus. "Are you coming with me?"

Do I have a choice? Don't answer that. Hey, do you think we could stop by the park while we're out? A little squirrel reconnaissance might be just what the doctor ordered. If we're going to ring that bell and there's the chance of wreaking havoc on the entire town, we might as well start with Skippy and his band of merry misfits. We simply don't know, but at least Skippy and his furry rat minions can be on the front line of any reaction. My diabolical doomsday destruction plan is finally coming together...two nemeses with one epic pawprint.

Chapter Five

W HAT EXACTLY DID *that experiment this afternoon tell us? I'll tell you what—it's very simple. We shouldn't go anywhere near the cemetery, especially the day before All Hallows' Eve.*

We'd spent a good half hour around lunch time ringing the bell, albeit hesitantly, in different spots around town. Lo and behold, the deepest tone occurred at the wrought-iron gate of our local cemetery. There had been no hide nor hair of Ivan, though I wasn't so sure I shouldn't have said scythe and hood, because his covert identity wasn't so off the record for us.

According to your favorite stick of wax, the grim reaper was out doing his duties today. I overheard that your favorite bank teller's mother kicked the bucket earlier today. He was probably haggling with the old bat over spare change. I hear his skills at the table aren't all that impressive.

"Leo," I admonished, feeling horrible for Nora. She was a sweet middle-aged lady who always took my bank deposit at the end of the day even if I was a couple minutes late to her window. "That's terrible."

The woman was a rickety and cranky ninety-nine-year-old woman who always sided with Skippy and his minions over the obvious dominant order of supernaturally inspired felines such as myself. Just last week, she shuffled out onto the porch waving a broomstick at me. She could move pretty fast for her age, that one.

She made it to the base of the old acorn tree in under two point five seconds. I've got to keep a close eye on Nora to make sure that she doesn't follow in her mother's footsteps. Skippy needs no more allies.

I could actually envision an elderly lady batting a broom on the sidewalk to make sure that Leo couldn't get anywhere near the local wildlife. It wasn't like Leo had the energy to actually run fast enough to catch anything, but Nora's mother had been playing it safe. I admired that trait, and I wonder just how her meeting had gone with good ol' Ivan.

We were currently in the living room of my cottage, getting ready for our meet and greet with said grim reaper. I could guess the only question on Leo's mind, but I had a million questions floating through mine. Ted had finally gotten the okay from Ivan to speak with me regarding our current predicament, and I wasn't sure if that was a good thing or a bad thing.

I can answer that question for you, if you'd like a realistic answer.

Ignoring Leo and walking to the kitchen, I began to clean up the dishes we'd left on the counter from dinner. Leo might continue to complain about this itsy-bitsy exploration into the cemetery's obvious involvement according to the bell, but he'd eventually cave. The temptation to secure an invite to the local supernatural poker game was just too hard to ignore.

My cottage was on the opposite side of town from the cemetery, which was probably a good thing given that the wrought iron gate in our front yard had been marked with a protection spell identifying those with suspicious intent. Well, it was not actually a true ward or a protection spell, exactly. It was more like an alarm system. The gate squeaked every time someone I didn't know or trust came through entrance. A true ward spell would cause physical damage to a troublemaker. A protection spell would prevent their entry.

Even I could admit that the exterior of the cottage was downright eerie looking, especially this time of year when the foliage had dropped. The interior? My Nan had style, it was that simple. She'd been a fashionista in her own right. She'd mixed a modern vibe with an antique style that had blended perfectly, and there wasn't a major design element I had changed since moving in. Besides, being surrounded by her own special touches made me feel closer to her.

We might be standing next to her in the afterlife if tonight doesn't go as planned. Speaking of plans, what is yours? I'm confusing myself with someone who matters, seeing as I'm just a casual observer here tonight.

"Leo, I can hear you complaining all the way in the bathroom," Heidi called out from where she was tucking her blonde hair into a black hat. She had some crazy idea that it would prevent Ivan from recognizing her in the future and holding a grudge against her that she was involved in this cesaral spirit bell caper. "I need a few more minutes to prepare."

I adjusted my black turtleneck, experiencing a bit of déjà vu. We'd dressed like this once before during a stroll through the cemetery, only to find an empty crypt that had been void of anything we'd expected to find. I was really hoping that a brief conversation with Ivan could enlighten us on why the bell kept ringing and the residents of Paramour Bay were seeing their long lost loved ones.

We technically already know the answer to that question, so we could essentially call off this so-called meet and greet with death.

"We do know that the veil is thin this time of year, but spirits normally don't go around showing themselves to just anyone," I argued, at a loss as to what type of spell I'd even be able to do to rectify this situation. I mean, we are talking the *other* world. I wasn't even sure an entire coven had the power to go up against something like that. "Look, we'll leave well enough alone if Ivan tells us that everything is fine without our intervention."

I have an idea. We can give the bell to him. I'll sacrifice a bit of my time to stay behind and show him how it works. Maybe shoot the bull for a little bit.

"You're just trying to wiggle your way into that poker game, aren't you?" I asked, not surprised when the doorbell rang. Ted said that he'd come to collect us when he was on his way back to the cemetery. "Did you forget that Ivan's host body is allergic to cats?"

I did not, which is why the family grimoire is currently on the coffee table and open to a page where you'll find a cat dander protection spell.

It didn't surprise me to know that Leo would go to great lengths in order to be a part of Ivan's weekly poker game. With that said, I wasn't so sure how a grim reaper would feel about a witch casting a spell on him.

"Ted, come on in," I said as I flung the door open. He was a stickler for manners, and never came in without an invitation. "Heidi isn't quite ready yet, so—"

Sweet angel of mercy, what in Hades is that abomination standing next to Ted?

That was the same basic question that had also formed in my mind, only I hadn't been able to vocalize it once I realized Ted was not alone.

Standing next to Ted was none other than my very own mother. That recent sense of déjà vu came back tenfold as I took in her appearance. Regina Lattice Marigold was once again dressed all in black, looking more like Elvira, Mistress of the Dark.

You mean, if the Mistress of the Dark was wearing leather pants and matching hipster boots. My eyes are burning, Raven. Make it stop.

"Good evening to you, too," my mother said wryly, not waiting for me to move from my frozen spot in front of the entrance. "Why is it that I had to hear from Beetle that the residents of this town are seeing their dead relatives, may they rest in peace?"

There's no peace to have when you look like an acolyte of the Manson family—

"Mrs. M, what are you doing here?" Heidi asked enthusiastically as she finally joined us, most likely having a good idea that she'd cut off one of Leo's not-so-nice quips. "Hey, I love those pants."

Why me?

Heidi was definitely laying it on thick, but her eagerness proved to be enough to steer my mother's interest from Leo back to her outfit. She turned her right leg inward, posing as she looked down at her favorite boots.

I feel a hairball forming at the back of my throat.

"Thank you, Heidi," my mother beamed before straightening and giving Leo a glare. So much for letting things go. Then again, Leo had been at fault for that one. "I'm here to make sure that the meeting with our local grim reaper goes off without a hitch. Those soul suckers can be downright tricky, from what I hear. This one can play a mean hand at poker, too. I couldn't believe my ears when Beetle explained what had been taking place recently. And don't even begin to think you can convince me that bell didn't warn you about this whole mess. Really,

Raven? A phone call saying that the cesaral spirit bell had been alerting you of random souls roaming around Paramour Bay would have been nice."

Nice would have been you staying in the city, but that didn't happen, either.

Ted continued to stand near the front door, his back ramrod straight as usual. He didn't particularly care for my mother, most likely having heard more than a few details from Leo rather than Nan about Mom leaving home to raise her daughter in the city. Ted had been very protective of my Nan. The hurt that remained when her only daughter chose to leave witchcraft behind had definitely left scars on everyone involved.

"Mom, there's nothing for you to worry about," I said, wishing that Beetle hadn't relayed the town's gossip to my mother over a phone call. He had no idea that we were witches, so it hadn't even crossed my mind that Beetle would end up calling my mother about something that he'd no doubt overheard at the diner. "You really should have called me first before driving all the way here. And how did you know that we were going to visit Ivan?"

"Why, I called Ted, of course," my mother exclaimed with a wave of her hand, as if that explained everything. It didn't. Not by a long shot. The two barely exchanged greetings, let alone an in-depth conversation about witchcraft. "Shall we get this meeting over with? I have plans with Beetle later."

Second hairball, coming right up.

"Ted, why didn't you tell me that you spoke with my mother?" I asked, flabbergasted that the question had even fallen off my lips. "I could have saved her a trip."

"Ms. Regina called the boutique this morning."

My mother didn't look the least bit guilty that she'd tracked

Ted down at the boutique, knowing full well that he'd be there paying a visit to the mannequin he'd fallen head over heels in love with since first laying eyes on her. I didn't even have to confirm that my mother asked him yes or no answers, thus allowing Ted to respond in short answers without Mindy or anyone figuring out what was being discussed over the phone.

Speaking of trips, can we free up your mother for her broom ride home?

"Mom, you really should just go on and enjoy your evening with Beetle," I suggested, though why I did so was beyond me. My mother claimed to have given up witchcraft, but Leo and I had already proven that to be a whopper of a self-serving fib. She'd clearly kept her pointy hat in the ring, and I'm pretty sure she was having a wee bit too much fun with these mysteries that she kept popping in on. "Heidi, Leo, and I are just going to ask Ivan a few discreet questions. We all know that the veil between us and the afterlife gets a bit thin this time of year. We're just being wary of complications, and simply talking about a few spirit sightings…nothing more than that."

One good thing about Beetle not knowing our little secret was that I was pretty much assured my mother had no idea how many times the cesaral spirit bell had rung recently. She'd be more likely to accept that only three sightings had occurred, which wasn't all that unusual around All Hallows' Eve.

We never thought to check for bugs. Not the eight-legged kind posing as eyelashes on Regina and Rowena's faces, but the listening kind that might be planted all around this cottage. I wouldn't put it past your mother, Raven. She might even have cameras.

Considering that Mom could hear every single word that Leo had just said, it wasn't a surprise that the two had begun arguing. I sighed in resignation and shot Heidi a look of gratitude. She'd tried to help, but this verbal altercation between my mother and Leo had been bound to happen. It was then I noticed the makeup underneath Heidi's eyes.

"Heidi, why do you look like a football player ready for kickoff?" I asked, having already guessed the answer. With that said, she'd gone above and beyond attempting to alter her appearance before meeting Ivan. "It's not like a grim reaper can come and snatch you up in the middle of the night. You are young, healthy, and probably won't pass into the afterlife until you're well into your old age."

"One can never be too careful," Heidi bantered back, patting her black knit cap that she'd stuffed her blonde hair into before adding the thick black lines of what had to be my regular eyeliner onto her cheeks. As far as I was aware, I hadn't had any greasepaint lying around in the bathroom. "So, what's the plan, Ted?"

Heidi's question finally drew Leo and my mother's attention away from one another. Ted shifted his weight in that uncomfortable manner of his when put under the spotlight, but he concisely summed up the brief meet and greet. It was barely long enough for Heidi to flash her cell phone at me.

My stomach reacted as if I were on a roller coaster, which was pretty close to the truth. With all these unexpected twists and turns this evening, I might as well have been strapped into the front seat. I'd completely forgotten that Liam had been meeting us out at the cemetery, but Heidi had thankfully diverted that so-called date for another time.

My mother had no idea that Liam knew the truth about our lineage.

I held my breath, hoping that Leo wouldn't remark on the sensitive topic, thereby cluing my mother in on our secret.

I get to add two additional items to my next catnip order. Agreed?

My mother did that perfected eyebrow arch thing of hers, catching on that Leo was basically blackmailing me over something or another. I didn't mind, though. Anything was better than receiving a long-winded lecture from my mother that would undeniably delay tonight's meeting unnecessarily.

"Fine," I relented, not really having a choice. Besides, I'd already seen the contents of the cart on the catnip site that was still up on my computer. He'd already added the items, knowing full well a time would come just like this that he'd be able to use to his advantage. "Now, what do you say, Mom? Go on and join Beetle for a late movie or something. We've got this covered."

My mother narrowed her eyes in suspicion, causing Leo to shudder in what I could only assume was the mere thought of spiders. A dull headache had begun to throb behind my temples, and we'd yet to even step one foot out the door.

Spiders rank right up there with clowns...creepy no matter which way you look at them.

"I think it's best I go with all of you," my mother replied stubbornly, which I'd already known and accepted her forthcoming negative response to my suggestion. She might still claim to not want anything to do with the supernatural, but she always managed to insert herself into the mysteries that kept Leo and I quite busy these days. "Ted, you can ride shotgun with me. I want to know all about your poker buddy, even his tells when he's trying to..."

Heidi, Leo, and I sighed as the odd pair finally left the house, fully expecting us to follow right behind. We were a bit slower in that task, grateful that the short car ride across town wouldn't be in the accompaniment of my mother.

I'm surprised she didn't arrive here on the backs of small children.

"You knew all along that your mother would be here, didn't you?" Heidi murmured, making sure that her voice didn't carry on the night air.

It was quite chilly, and I was grateful that I hadn't changed out of my black turtleneck. I'd already grabbed my jacket from the coatrack before closing the door behind us. I doubt that we'd be at the cemetery long, but it was better to be safe than sorry.

"Mom's habit of showing up unexpectedly isn't so surprising anymore," I said wryly, watching as Ted tried to squeeze his large frame into the compact vehicle. "She might continue to deny practicing witchcraft, but having her by our side while meeting the grim reaper might not be such a bad idea. She's been at this much longer than I have. She might be useful."

You're right, Raven. Maybe we should consider making a deal of some sort—a bit of information in exchange for good ol' Ivan to give your mother an express ticket on the cool chute to Hades. I bet he'd get points for collecting her soul. I never considered it before, but there's a good chance that Regina is on Hades' ten most wanted list. Go figure. The possibilities for tonight's meeting are finally looking up!

Chapter Six

I T WAS HARD to stop the shivers of unease that traveled over my body from head to toe at the sight of that slightly crooked wrought-iron gate in front of the cemetery. Understandably, there was something very foreboding about standing in front of a graveyard the night before All Hallows' Eve. Low patches of fog wove its way through tombstones of all different shapes and sizes. Truthfully, the older ones that were worn with age or cracked and sitting at a bit of an odd angle gave me the heebie-jeebies.

It wasn't as if the plots were so bad that they needed immediate attention. Keeping in mind a reaper was in fact the groundskeeper at our cemetery, it appeared to be maintained on a fairly regular basis; regardless, there were still indicators that this graveyard had been around for quite a while. The spooky vibe was intensified due to a few of the tombstones having moss climbing over some of the marble surfaces, yet the grass was freshly mowed. I guess that wasn't surprising, given that this place was full of contradictions.

"Did I ever tell you about the time I snuck into a graveyard with Tommy Poplar back in high school?" Heidi asked in a low whisper, skimming the first row of tombstones with the powerful beam of her flashlight. "We—"

I used the back of my hand to smack Heidi on the arm, once

again experiencing a very strong sense of déjà vu. Even Leo couldn't contain a groan of misery regarding the last time we'd visited the cemetery at night, only to find a crypt that was empty yet full of mystery.

I can only take so much, and a few quick tokes off my catnip pipe is only going to last so long. Don't jinx us with talk of empty crypts and memories of soul-eating ghouls…unless one wants to drain the lifeforce from your mother. If that's the case, I'm all for summoning up the undead. Maybe Skippy has a recon group in the area.

"This way, Miss Raven."

Ted's formal tone had startled all of us. He hadn't whispered or used a subdued tone, but instead spoke as if we were having a conversation in the middle of the day on the main street of town. I wasn't sure why people felt the urge to speak softly in a cemetery, especially at night. It wasn't like the dead could be awakened by our conversations. In fact, maybe those left behind might enjoy the opportunity to overhear a discussion.

My mother had already parted the semi-rusted wrought-iron gate and was waiting for us just inside the entrance to the cemetery grounds. I could see the slight interest in tonight's escapade by the sparkles in her emerald green eyes. The nearly full moon was giving off enough light that we technically didn't need the flashlights.

Oddly enough, I hadn't noticed before now that All Hallows' Eve would have a full moon this year. That had to have some significance when it came to our current ghost invasion. Having once before descended into one of the crypts lining the back of the cemetery, I wasn't taking any chances. There were plenty of dark niches around here.

"Ted, where is it exactly that you play poker?" I asked, the last to join in on our single-file march into the graveyard. Leo had made sure that he was tucked safely in between Heidi and me. "In one of the crypts?"

My position in line is very strategic, Raven. I spent the car ride over here going over our approach and options for a marching order. We can increase our chances of survivability by weaving through the tombstones. The reason being is that your mother would sacrifice me in one blink of those spider eyes of hers. Two, Ted moving in any direction is like watching molasses drip down the side of a pancake in the dead of winter. Heidi loves me, and you have a tendency to throw an energy ball in random directions at the slightest hint of danger, clearly evident by the time you tried to melt Ted by hitting him in the chest with that horrifying defensive move. My best odds are right between you and Heidi, provided that Skippy doesn't join the party. In that case, I'd have to go with option B.

"Don't you dare ask that ragamuffin what option B is, Raven," my mother warned from her position in between Ted and Heidi. She'd slipped in behind Ted when he'd taken the lead through the cemetery without hesitation or consultation. I wasn't even sure that Ted had a fight or flight instinct. "Leo, you haven't shut up since we got here. Put a sock in it or pipe down so that I can listen to our surroundings. Raven, you should do the same. Tune into your senses and take heed of any intuition that strikes you at a moment's notice."

Leo had abruptly stopped in front of me, crouching down low with his hefty butt stuck up and wiggling in the air. My mother had upset him, and he was now getting ready to pounce without thinking of the consequences. His self-preservation had gone out the window, and it just went to show how rattled he was that we were creeping through the cemetery with the intention of meeting the grim reaper. I knelt down and gently put my hand on his back as the others continued forward.

"You did start this squabble with Mom by saying you wouldn't care if she got eaten by a soul-eating ghoul," I reminded him with a smirk. I also used this time to do as my mother suggested, focusing all of my attention on our surroundings. "Let this one go, especially since we're about to finally meet Ivan. Besides, she's trying to help me learn something here."

Leo huffed, his right eye narrowing in what could only be described as a slightly delayed glare of retribution.

Fine. I'll just ante up your mother's soul into the pot when it comes to upping the stakes in a hand that I'll purposefully throw Ivan's way. Maybe it will sweeten him up and get me included on the weekly roster.

Ted, Heidi, and my mother were now quite a bit ahead of us. One would think given the eerie atmosphere of the graveyard, it would have had me scurrying ahead to catch them. Instead, I took my mother's advice to heart. By standing here with Leo, I was able to hear more distant sounds than just our footsteps crunching through the grass below our shoes.

What you're hearing is me grinding my teeth, which I can't afford to do with this crooked deciduous canine of mine. On the bright side, I don't have Ted's choppers.

"Is there something different about the cemetery tonight?" I asked cautiously, purposefully keeping my voice soft so that my words didn't carry through the chilly night air. I couldn't pinpoint exactly what I was picking up, but the palm of my hand definitely began to generate heat the longer we stood in one spot. "Where are the sounds of the crickets or frogs like last time?"

Would you stick around this place with a grim reaper lurking about or worse…your mother? She could knock a squirrel out of a tree at fifty paces on just looks alone.

I was keeping an eye on the others when I noticed Heidi glance over her shoulder, probably to inquire about something to do with Ivan. Either that, or she was going to comment about zombie hands popping up throughout graveyard.

Heidi does have a fear of such thing, doesn't she? She has no idea that the woman in front of her is far worse than any flesh-eating zombie, even the black plague.

Heidi almost stumbled when she saw how far back we were, but the terrified squeal that came from her throat was due to something...more like someone...walking past one of the tombstones and disappearing into thin air. I wouldn't have believed that I'd seen the apparition myself if I hadn't witnessed Heidi's reaction, too. It was that fleeting.

Are you sure it wasn't Skippy? That hairy rat was the one who snatched my attention away from the empty crypt the last time we were here, remember? For all I know, Skippy is a regular at their poker game. He's squirrelly like that.

"It wasn't Skippy," I murmured warily, turning in a full circle to make sure nothing else was sneaking up on us that would cause either of us to scream in full-on panic. Heidi's tiny squeal meant she was close to freaking out, even though she was usually the one to forge ahead in these instances. Well, that was before she knew about the supernatural world with witches, ghosts, and grim reapers. "It's a little late, but I'm now reconsidering our decision to leave the bell at home. Maybe we should have brought it with us."

Have you ever heard of the saying that what you can't see won't hurt you? I believe that applies in this case. Come to think of it, have you considered cloaking your mother? That would solve a lot of our problems. Out of sight, out of mind.

"That's just because it fits your narrative."

I'm glad that Leo hadn't pushed the Skippy theory, because if the cute little squirrel had shown up in the cemetery, Leo would have likely gone running off into the dark chasing his own shadow. The last thing I needed was to lose track of him with all these spirits running about. Who knows what they thought of necromancy, but my first assumption would be jealousy. Maybe outright hatred.

Leo's gasp of horror had me peering down at him, only to realize that he'd heard every word in my head. Even after a full year had passed, I still sometimes forgot that he could hear every thought that passed through my brain. A quick look toward Heidi assured me that my mother and Ted had squashed any panic that might have resulted in her seeing an apparition wandering through the graveyard. Now, I needed to fix my mistake so that we could finally get to our meeting with Ivan.

"Leo, I didn't really mean that the spirits are jealous of you or that they might dislike you. You're safe, and—"

Sweet angel of mercy, I'm going to die! I knew following your mother here was a mistake.

"Leo, you're not going to die." I knelt once more with every intention of stroking Leo's back in reassurance, but he was having none of that. He'd jumped two feet backwards to avoid my touch, totally aghast that he hadn't considered the effect a recipient might have from a necromancy spell in this type of scenario. "These spirits probably have no idea that a necromancy spell was used to keep you from crossing into the afterlife."

You don't know that! You're just saying that so I don't go into a full-blown asthma attack. What if they've all come through the thin veil to exact their revenge on me for being the one who made it through with hardly any adverse consequences?

I literally had to bite my tongue and think of coffee so that

Leo wouldn't hear the laundry list of residual effects that wanted to immediately spring to mind about his appearance and short-term memory.

I still have things to do, Raven. The squirrelpocalypse is practically upon us, and I'm the only one who is taking that even remotely seriously! And don't even get me started on your lessons, because who knows what type of student you'd be if your witchcraft were left in your mother's hands. If Regina had her way, she'd cast a spell on you where she wiped out the last twelve months of your memory. All my hard work and patience…for nothing!

I attempted to figure out the best way to convince Leo that my imagination had gone into overdrive and there were no spirits who were seeking revenge, but the strangled noise that came from his throat all but told me I was about to be dealing with something worse than stopping his asthma attack.

Whatever you do, Raven, don't look behind you.

Leo's left eye was focused on something directly over my right shoulder, and I couldn't help myself. Who could in a situation like this?

A reasonably smart person who has a detectable measure of self-preservation, that's who!

The temptation was just too much, and I'd already shifted in my favorite knee-high boots I might never get to wear again should the grim reaper standing before me decide to strike me down into one of these graves.

What's in Ivan's hand? I knew it! I knew it! It's express tickets to Hades, and we're not even packed! Brace yourself, Raven. It's going to be a long, hot, bumpy ride!

Chapter Seven

*W*ELL, THAT WAS *an epic letdown. This is Ivan? I've got to hand it to him...that smile is downright creepy.*

Once I'd stopped Leo from going into a full-blown asthma attack, he'd looked beyond the deck of cards in Ivan's hands to see the weathered face of an elderly gentleman. It was true that there was a spine-chilling grin gracing his lips, but that was to be expected given the drawings I'd seen during my research on grim reapers.

In occult history, grim reapers were usually depicted as skeletal remains and adorned in black robes. They held a scythe in their hands and had red, glowing eyes that were unmistakable and synonymous for death. It was also said that they could inhabit a recently vacated human body and walk the earth...which was apparently true given that we were witnessing one in person.

I believe I might be losing my interest in playing in that weekly poker game. Hey, Raven. Can Ivan hear me? If not, let him know that I just realized I give myself a bath every Wednesday night and will be unavailable to play. Can't let my hygiene go, now can I?

"Um, you must be Ivan," I managed to say after clearing my throat a couple of times. I'd taken a couple steps back out of self-preservation. By this time, Heidi had run to my side and grabbed ahold of my hand. My mother wasn't so quick on her feet, but she did cautiously approach us while keeping a vigilant watch on Ivan. As for Ted, he casually followed suit as if Ivan was nothing more than a seventy-something year old groundskeeper. "It's nice to finally meet you."

Really? Did you just tell a grim reaper that you were glad to meet him? There is seriously something wrong with the way your brain makes connections, Raven.

"Miss Marigold," Ivan replied, his gravelly bass voice as disturbing as his smile. I swallowed back my panic, reminding myself that I'd sought out this meeting and that it wasn't my time to be escorted into the afterlife. "I hadn't planned on meeting you for quite some time yet. It's an honor to make your acquaintance beforehand."

Does he mean that you and I are going to be here for a while? Remember, I have plans to stop the squirrelpocalypse. That counts for something on the old balance scale, right?

"Mr. Leo, you have nothing to fear from me this evening." While the grim reaper was known for his glowing red eyes, Ivan's was an uncanny blue that reminded me of a clear sky on a summer afternoon. Those baby blues focused intently on Leo. It wasn't a surprise when he lifted one of his claws and sunk them deep into the leather of my boot. "Should your pupil come up with an appropriate spell to help with this body's allergies, I'm sure we can come to an agreement about reserving a spot for you at our weekly poker game. Unless, of course, your vital grooming routine cannot be moved to another night."

"Ivan can hear your thoughts, Leo," I whispered, just in case he'd missed it over my mother's casual chuckle. It was quite disturbing, but she seemed rather comfortable in the grim reaper's presence. "You might want to watch your sense of humor around him."

Give me a moment, Raven. I'm verklempt. The grim reaper addressed me properly, Raven. I'm so overcome with emotion that I may just allow him to scratch behind my ears.

It would be just my luck that Ivan had utilized the one manner in which to get Leo on his side. I had been worried I'd missed one of the occult objects that I'd discovered in the antique shop a couple of months ago. I had even stopped in this afternoon to have a quick look around, but I hadn't been able to find a thing related to the supernatural. What I hadn't seriously considered was the grim reaper being the one responsible. What if he had ulterior motives?

Heidi's breathing had evened out a bit, but she still maintained a fierce grip on my hand. I didn't mind, though. The thing about having a best friend was that you knew they'd go down swinging with the very last play in the game.

Speaking of games, Mr. Ivan, I would be honored to join you and the others in your weekly poker game. After we clear up a few things, we can go about ridding that human vessel of yours of those pesky cat allergies. All in all, this evening is turning out to be quite splendid.

"Oh, knock it off," I told Leo in irritation, figuring it was just my luck to have Leo side with a possible adversary. "Ivan, don't let Leo fool you with his proper tone. He's a card shark and will take all your money when you least expect it, but he does in fact have a heart of gold."

Sweet angel of mercy, do you want me to be penciled in on his appointment calendar?

"I assure you, Mr. Leo, your name is not on my list for this evening." Ivan took his time in meeting everyone's gaze before finally focusing on me, although he did seem to concentrate on my mother longer than necessary. It was only then that her cool composure seemed to fracture a bit. I'm not sure Ivan even noticed now that he was shuffling the deck in his hands. It was oddly mesmerizing to see the knotted knuckles gracefully rearrange and create a bridge with the cards. "What is it that you need help with, Miss Marigold?"

This was it—showtime. My shining moment in talking with an actual grim reaper. I forced my shoulders to relax, somewhat reassured that we were all safe from being escorted into the afterlife this evening.

"I'm sure that Ted has already told you what has been happening with the residents around town. I was hoping you could give us some insight as to why such occurrences are taking place in Paramour Bay."

Ivan didn't reply right away, but instead continued to smile as he pondered my request. There was a part of me that sensed he was debating on telling me the truth, which confounded me. Unless, of course, he was the one responsible.

Don't utter such blasphemy!

"Miss Marigold, I don't like to meddle in affairs that don't affect me," Ivan ended up replying after a long pause. He continued to shuffle the cards as if he had all the time in the world. I guess given his job, he *did* have all the time in the world. "With that said, you might want to look closer to home."

"Are you saying that I somehow missed an object at the antique shop?" I asked, having already ruled out that possibility this afternoon. Unless…

Inventory! Why didn't we think of that? Mr. Ivan, you're a genius! Isn't he, Raven? The antique shop must have something in the storage room that Lydia or Kathleen haven't displayed for their customers. Well, now that we have that taken care of, let's get on with this allergy-ridding incantation, shall we?

"Um, may I ask a question?" Heidi inquired, sounding like she had a horrible case of laryngitis. I had to hold back a laugh when I realized she didn't want Ivan to know the sound of her voice. I'm pretty sure it didn't matter, but there was no convincing her any differently. "How doesn't it affect you when a spirit comes back through the veil?"

"Miss Connolly, I—"

"Who's Miss Connolly?" Heidi asked in a feigned shocked manner, even looking around her as if someone else might have joined the group. She hadn't been successful in the least in diverting Ivan's attention away from her true identity. It was better to let her believe it worked, allowing her that false sense of security. "A mix-up, I'm sure. You were saying?"

Sometimes I do wonder about the motives of my beloved Heidi. Mr. Ivan, please continue.

Ivan blinked slowly as he realized it was best to follow Leo's advice and just to go along with the program. His creepy smile was still in place, though.

"As I was saying, my duties are complete when I escort the spirits to the other side," Ivan shared, not telling us anything we didn't already know. "What they do afterward is not my concern."

I like the way you do business, Mr. Ivan—only what the contract stipulates.

I'd come to know a lot about the paranormal during my research, and I was reminded in this moment that some supernatural entities only answered specifically when a proper inquiry was asked. We needed to reword the question.

Do we really, though? We could technically call this a win-win with you planning to go by the antique shop tomorrow while I join in tonight's poker game. Think this through, Raven. Don't rain on my parade.

"Ivan, who is responsible for allowing the spirits to return to our world?" I was pretty pleased with myself when Ivan nodded his head in encouragement.

"The only way a spirit can return in the manner you're suggesting is through very powerful magic."

So, it *was* an occult object that I'd overlooked in the antique shop. It was a good thing that Beetle was minding the shop tomorrow morning, because I planned on visiting Lydia to see if I could have a peek at the items in the storage room or a list of any suspect sales she may have made.

And there you have it, Raven. Okay, off you go! Don't wait up. Oh, wait. You need to do one itsy-bitsy allergy-blocking spell before you do. Not that I need to remind you, but now is not the time for any unforced errors, either.

"I don't believe that bit about powerful magic to be true, Ivan," my mother interjected, even causing Ted's eyes to widen with disbelief that my mother would question the wisdom of a grim reaper. By this point, Leo sounded as if one of his asthma attacks had been triggered. "What about all those sightings of apparitions by mere humans? Or the hauntings of houses and places that we so often hear about, Ivan? Surely those spirits have no access to magic on our side of the veil."

What is this? A Paranormal 101 class? Get her to stop, Raven. Right now!

"You are, of course, speaking of those souls who refuse to cross over, Ms. Marigold." Ivan had stopped shuffling the deck of cards in his hand, which told me he was okay with Leo's thought on bringing this conversation to an end. "They are stuck in the middle, sorting through their affairs until they decide they would like to avail themselves to my services. There is not much to be done about those troubled souls until only they decide otherwise. Now, if there isn't anything else, I do believe it is time for my favorite activity of the week."

"Thank you, Ivan," my mother murmured, unexpectedly stepping forward and placing her hand on Ivan's arm. I'm pretty sure that Heidi, Leo, and I all gasped in horror at her forwardness. Ivan didn't seem to mind, though. "I do so appreciate your discretion."

I somehow got lost in this conversation, but I really don't care at this point. Raven, would you kindly cast the allergy-blocking spell so that I may live out my fantasy of winning my catnip money from the other supernatural beings in this town? Opportunities like this one only come around every so often. Ted, hand over the herbs so that we can get our game on.

"I like your enthusiasm, Mr. Leo," Ivan commended with that disturbing smile. I'd bet on him knowing full well that he was just stoking Leo's fire. I wasn't going to hear the end of these weekly poker games for years to come. "I'm all yours, Miss Marigold."

Chop-chop, Raven. My time has finally come.

My mother stepped back, seemingly content with how this meeting had gone. Heidi appeared reluctant to release my hand, but she finally relented when Ted stepped forward with the two herbs needed for this particular spell—a sprig of nettle and a pinch of goldenrod flower. Truthfully, I'm not quite sure that Ivan was ready to tangle with Leo when he was in this type of mood, but it was better than being cooped up with him on the car ride home.

"You should know that this incantation will only temporarily block your allergies," I informed him, not surprised when I caught sight of our so-called cousin crossing the graveyard. Rye must have parked back by the old family crypts that lined the edge of the property. "If you'd like to continue to invite Leo to your weekly get-togethers, I can let Rye know what the brief verbal component is to cast the spell."

If? What in the Hades are you suggesting? Why would you even contemplate that my good friend here wouldn't want me to have a permanent seat at his weekly poker game? I'll be the life of the party with all my war stories of how I'm stopping the forthcoming squirrelpocalypse, Raven.

"I look forward to hearing your plans, Mr. Leo," Ivan said, giving Leo the reassurance he needed in regard to joining his super-secret supernatural group. As I quickly cast the spell, he did say something that was rather odd and looked at my mother in the process. Honestly, it made absolutely no sense to me. "It should be noted that although this body may be spelled, that of my entity may not."

Why would Ivan warn me about something like that? Did he think that I would actually try and use magic on a grim reaper? Had my mother? Let's face it. Ivan had the ability to escort us through the veil. I wasn't even close to being ready in joining the afterlife.

I'm not letting this ruin my evening, Raven. My good friend might simply have wanted to state a simple fact without there being any untoward meaning behind it. As for you, resident warlock, prepare to lose the shirt off your back. Ted, keep your shirt on...I'll just want the jacket to sleep on.

"Let's do this then," Rye said as he rubbed his hands together in anticipation. Oh, I was definitely going to hear all the scuttlebutt about this poker game. Leo was about to have the time of his life. "And don't think for a second that your premium catnip can replace the Benjamins. Not going to happen."

Leo happily fell beside Rye as the two continued to banter about what was acceptable to put into the pot, with Ted following behind in his methodical manner. I then met Ivan's gaze, nodding my appreciation for his time. I'm not sure how a grim reaper went about blocking out a few hours every Wednesday to host a poker game, and it was best not to ask.

"Good luck, Miss Marigold," Ivan said with a slight nod in return. "As for you, Miss Connolly, you'll be happy to know that you are not on my list for this evening, either."

The black lines of grease on Heidi's cheeks made her blue eyes stand out even more. It made her blinking in astonishment easier to see as she digested Ivan's meaning.

"If I may ask, what about tomorrow? I mean, do you receive a list hourly? Daily? Weekly? I'm not admitting to being Heidi Connolly, but is there a way for you to glance at a calendar for the next couple of decades on her behalf? I can totally relay that message for you. I'm sure the two of you can even come to some sort arrangement in exchange for that information. I mean, Ivan—the body you borrowed—still has to pay taxes. I'm sure that I could—I mean, Heidi—give you free tax services for as long as you'd like. What do you say, Ivan?"

My mother rolled her eyes at Heidi's ability to speak three times as fast in stressful situations and took her by the arm with every intention of leading her to the front of the graveyard where we'd parked our vehicles. Ivan was able to relay one more piece of advice that I did believe we should all take to heart…that was, if there wasn't some object in Paramour Bay causing long-lost loved ones to somehow cross through the veil.

"Miss Connolly, each day is a gift. Live each second to the fullest, leaving behind no regrets. This is true should I be your escort tomorrow or when you are ninety-two, three months, and two days old. You must always remember that there are no guarantees."

The sound of those cards being shuffled in Ivan's hand was the only thing carrying through the chilly night air as he walked off into the darkness, following the others to whatever secret place they'd set aside for a night of supernatural poker.

"Heidi, dear," my mother began, her green eyes shimmering with mischief now that the three of us were alone. As a matter of fact, she seemed very happy at the moment. "Did the grim reaper just tell you when it will be your time to be escorted into the afterlife?"

"Maybe," Heidi replied cautiously, seeming to be breathing a little bit easier now that we weren't standing directly in front of Death. "What did the *no guarantee* thing mean, though? Did that mean my death wasn't carved in stone? Could that change? Or do you think he was just toying with me?"

"Our local grim reaper did seem the type to have a dark sense of humor, did he not?" My mother had linked her arm with Heidi's, turning her to face the front of the cemetery so they could begin their walk through the tombstones. "I think Leo might have met his match. Did you notice that…"

I let the two of them go ahead of me, needing a moment to sort through the conversation we'd just had with a grim reaper. Dealing personally with Death certainly wasn't an everyday occurrence, so my fear might have prevented me from analyzing the entire discussion. One thing stood out, though, and that was the fact that I was to look close to home for whatever magical item could be responsible for allowing spirits to cross through the veil.

First thing tomorrow, I was going to stop by the antique

shop and convince Lydia that I needed to take a quick look around the storage room. I wasn't quite sure what explanation I could give her that wouldn't make me seem like I was a bit off my rocker or one of those people obsessed with the occult, but I would figure it out over a cup of coffee in the morning. My cup of sanity had a way of making everything right in the world.

In the meantime, I was going to have to ask my mother not to keep Beetle out too late tonight since I needed him to open the shop tomorrow. I cringed just thinking about having that awkward chat. My mother seemed to delight in my awkwardness, but it must be done...for the sake of the residents in Paramour Bay.

Something flickered in my peripheral vision, giving me pause. It must have been my imagination, because Mom and Heidi didn't seem to notice anything out of the ordinary. I still slowed my pace to carefully look around the graveyard, noticing that the patches of fog had become quite thick in our short time talking to Ivan. Upon arriving, the palm of my right hand had begun to harness a bit of heat. Even though I could now sense piercing tingles, I couldn't make out any sign of a threat to our safety.

Was I just stressing over the fact that All Hallows' Eve or my birthday celebration might not quite go as planned? Tomorrow was my favorite time of the year, and this was the first time that I would be able to celebrate it with the man who'd swept me off my feet, my best friend, and the new ones I'd made in a town I now called home. I had a lot to be thankful for, and I wanted the day to go off without a hitch. I should probably rephrase that, because first thing tomorrow would find me at the antique shop.

I had an easy task in front of me, right?

All I had to do was locate the occult object that was somehow allowing spirits to slip through the veil between us and the afterlife.

Easy-peasy, lemon squeezy.

Chapter Eight

"**I**SN'T THIS CROSSING some line that you're going to be uncomfortable with?" I asked Liam, keeping my voice low so that Eileen couldn't overhear us. His dispatcher was the official eyes and ears of this town, but thankfully the supernatural events that had occurred recently had all flown under the radar. "I didn't stop by with the intention to talk you into going over to the antique shop with me. I just wanted to keep you informed of what I intended to do, and maybe entice a kiss of encouragement from you this morning."

Oddly enough, the bell hadn't rung once after I'd returned to the cottage. I'd spent a couple of hours before bed waiting for the inevitable toll, but all had been silent. Maybe whatever object was still at the antique shop had been depleted of its magic. Heidi had agreed and driven home in her "new" used car, acquired since her move from New York City, still mulling over Ivan's riddle. My mother had chosen to stay the night with Beetle, that slight edge to her evaporating into the chilly night air.

As for Leo, I'm pretty sure I heard him and Ted return home at around two o'clock this morning, having overindulged in whatever supernatural companionship they all shared. I wasn't sure what types of drinks were served at an otherworldly poker game, but I'm relatively certain from the knick-knacks hitting the floor one by one that Leo had snuck in some of his premium organic catnip edibles. If it were possible, he was even less graceful when he'd consumed too much of his treat of choice.

Would you mind lowering the volume of your thoughts, birthday girl? My head is pounding like a jackhammer, the glaring sunlight coming through the window hurts my left eye, and the smell of that crazy dispatcher's perfume makes me want to hurl. My plan to stop the squirrelpocalypse will have to wait a day while I try to figure out who spiked my edibles. My bet is on our resident warlock. He seemed to turn up with one full boat after another at just the right times to rake the larger pots.

"I'm not crossing any lines if finding that object and casting a warding spell on it keeps this town safe," Liam replied, freezing in place before he stood up from his chair. "Wow. I never thought I'd catch myself saying something like that in the line of duty."

"You did say that I kept your life exciting," I teased, tilting my face for a kiss when he finally made his way around his desk. "I'll take that kiss now."

Leo purposefully gagged in that dramatic flair of his, though he still remained invisible due to Eileen's presence in the outer area. Liam was fully aware of Leo and all of his idiosyncrasies.

Between the heavy dose of perfume wafting in the air and your so-called public displays of affection, I'm not responsible for the hairball that I'm about to produce. You might call it the mother of all hairballs. You know, it just hit me—Ted has been known to surprise us a time or two. Maybe he was the one who spiked my edibles, wanting to change his luck at the table. It's always the quiet ones we have to watch out for, you know.

Liam drew me into the warmth of his embrace, pressing his soft lips to mine as his woodsy scent surrounded me. Going in search of a magical item that was literally turning Paramour Bay into a ghost town wasn't exactly how I'd planned on getting a head start on my birthday. I'd needed this little private time for reassurance that today would end on a positive note.

A positive note would be you doing me a huge favor to make this catnip hangover disappear. Did you get a chance to look up a spell for hangovers like I asked? I don't think I can get through the day with this raging case of cottonmouth. It's like someone shoved a ball of the stuff down my throat and wired my jaw shut. Hey, you don't think my good friend would have done such a thing as to spike my edibles, do you? I was sitting to Mr. Ivan's left, and he is left-handed.

I pulled away from Liam with a sigh, resting my forehead against his chest for just another second of sanity. Leo had been complaining all morning about how someone had done something to his treats, because that was the only way to ensure that he wouldn't rake in all the chips last night.

"Leo, we talked about this," I muttered, looking over my shoulder at one of the guest chairs. I had no doubt it was the one that Leo had plopped on when I'd made him come with me this morning. He was well-rounded in occult objects, so he might be able to identify some of the inventory at the antique shop that I might accidentally overlook. "We shouldn't use magic for self-gain. We must suffer the consequences of our actions."

"Do I even want to know what that's about?" Liam asked with a chuckle, reaching behind him for his badge. He'd changed from having the pinned badge on his khaki shirt to the leather backed flip model with an attached chain to hang it around his neck. It made it easier to see when he wore his bomber jacket due to the colder weather this time of year. He could just pull it out and wear it at a scene, if needed. "Don't answer that. There are some things that I just shouldn't know."

You throwing my words back at me isn't going to work this time, Raven. Think of it as being for the greater good of this town. How am I supposed to be on my game in searching for this alleged object in question you think is still at the antique shop when I can't even open my eyes to look for it?

"You're bound to find out," I answer Liam wryly, still ignoring Leo's request. It was his own fault that he'd consumed too much premium organic catnip at last night's poker game. It was a lesson learned, and he would absolutely be saying the same thing to me had I hit the wine bottle too hard. "Leo was invited to stay for last night's game. Let's just say that he lost track of time and hit the catnip a bit too hard, and he's now paying the price."

"Ahhh, the infamous poker game hangover," Liam said in commiseration. He dropped a kiss on my forehead, surprising me with a request. "Would you mind keeping Eileen busy while I have a moment alone with Leo?"

Wait just a squirrel's chatter. Did the good ol' sheriff just request to speak with me in private? I don't know about this, Raven. I'm not in the proper frame of mind to be dealing with some sort of intervention…or asking for your hand in marriage. Neither subject is going to work for me. I'm forewarning you now. My answer is a resounding no to both. N. O. No. Oh, my nausea is returning full force. Why is the room spinning?

"Good luck," I said, wondering what in the world Liam had in mind. Although we've known each other for a year, we'd only been dating ten months. We weren't anywhere near ready for marriage, so that thought hadn't even entered my mind. I did think it was sweet that Leo would want to give approval for my hand in marriage, though. "Leo, show yourself so that Liam isn't talking to a chair."

I held back a laugh when Leo materialized, looking a lot worse for wear than he had when I'd woken up this morning. I'm not sure how I missed it earlier, but I'm pretty sure there was leftover catnip stuck to his face. He'd risen up to sit on his haunches, and there was now a slight sway to his upper body.

"I've got this," Liam reassured me, though I wasn't too sure what he meant by that. It wasn't like he could understand a word Leo said, so it was pretty much going to be a one-sided conversation. "Don't worry, Raven. We'll only be a minute."

I wasn't going to say that I wasn't curious as to why Liam wanted a moment alone with Leo, but I wasn't going to deny him this request. After how he'd handled the big supernatural reveal, I could give him this small appeal.

"Are you two off to a birthday breakfast?" Eileen asked with a twinkle in her eye. She leaned forward so that the pumpkin's green tassel on her shirt rested on the desk. Everyone knew of her propensity to wear outrageous holiday sweaters, but it was still shocking to the eye to actually be in the room with one of her favorites. "I can't wait to hear what you think of your birthday present, dear. Liam was so excited that he had to show me earlier this week. I'm surprised you didn't hear my squeal of delight all the way over at the tea shop."

I couldn't stop the faint flush of my cheeks upon hearing that Liam had bought me a birthday present. I mean, I figured he would, especially considering that he was the one who was technically throwing me the small get-together at the pub after the town's trick or treating extravaganza. But it still warmed my heart to hear that he was excited about whatever it was he'd gotten me.

"You wouldn't want to give me a small hint, now would

you?" I whispered in earnest, leaning in close just in case Eileen couldn't contain herself. After all, Liam *had* instructed me to keep Eileen distracted while he had a brief conversation with Leo. "Did he say where he was when he—"

"Do I want to know why the two of you have your heads together as if you're devising a plan to abscond with all the kids' candy tonight?" Liam asked, having come out of his office a lot quicker than I'd anticipated. He couldn't have said more than ten words to Leo, who had yet to utter a word. I tried to stifle the guilt that slid over my emotions. "Just so you know, the Payday candy bars are all mine."

"You mean you're offering a quarter to each child who sneaks you one when their parents aren't looking." Eileen laughed until the eyes of the pumpkins lit up on her sweater. When Leo didn't comment on such an outlandish display, I worried that he might have actually choked on that hairball he kept claiming was stuck in the back of his throat. "You didn't hear this from me, but I heard Monty was handing out Paydays over at his shop this year."

"He might already be a few bags shy of those treats," Liam confessed with a grin, resting his hand on my lower back. "Listen, we're heading over to the antique shop. There's a rare artifact that went missing in New Haven, and I told Sergeant Kiernan that I'd check in with the local shops to see if anyone tried to pawn it off as an old family heirloom."

"Ah, I get it." Eileen nodded in approval, though I think I missed something unspoken that had occurred between the two of them. "You're dragging Raven along so that Lydia doesn't keep asking you about Kathleen's case."

Technically, there really wasn't a case against Kathleen Reynolds. Long story short, she co-owned the antique shop across the street. Believing that her brother-in-law had been cheating on her sister, Kathleen had put a few drops of licorice oil into his tea. That particular component was rumored to be a truth serum of sorts. She'd had no idea that her brother-in-law had been allergic to it, causing him to drop dead in the middle of town square.

Liam had been in close contact with one of the prosecutors, and everyone was in agreement that it had been nothing short of a tragic accident. There would probably be no charges against Kathleen seeing as she had no intent to harm anyone, but Lydia was a worrier nonetheless. With that said, Eileen had jumped to a conclusion as to why I was tagging along with Liam.

"Something like that," Liam said vaguely, but with a smile. He didn't like to stretch the truth, but instead preferred to be honest and upfront. Unfortunately, the truth about my lineage and my gift were causing him to have to alter his approach ever so slightly. We both agreed it was for the greater good. Besides, we did believe that there was an artifact that didn't belong at the antique shop, and it could very well have come from New Haven. "I'll be back soon."

Liam opened the front door of the police station, motioning for me to go ahead of him. The crisp air hit me square in the face, but it was rather refreshing. I'd been worried about rain ruining this All Hallows' Eve, but the meteorologist had assured the public this morning that our area would get a respite from the incoming storm front until well after midnight.

I don't know about you, but isn't this day just grand? After our visit to the antique shop, I think I'll go see how Skippy's little operation is going over at the park.

I could literally hear Leo take a deep breath as we walked down the sidewalk to the cobblestone crosswalk.

Do you smell that wonderful scent, Raven? Someone is burning some firewood. Doesn't that just get you into the Halloween spirit? What a beautiful morning it is, and I have the good ol' sheriff to thank for it. I fear I might have been too harsh of a critic this past year, so you'll have to extend my apologies.

"What did you say to Leo back in your office, and where did my cantankerous hungover familiar go when I wasn't looking?" I murmured, waving to Candy as she made her way to the salon. She had a box of donuts that she must have acquired at Bree's bakery. "I might have to make him an appointment with Dr. Jameson."

Can't a familiar simply be in a good mood? Why do you have to go and ruin it with mentioning that doctor associated with the V word, Raven? Way to go, birthday girl. Just pour your poison in someone else's ear.

"No need to call the vet," Liam said with a laugh, though it faded quickly the closer we got to Candy on the other side of the street. "I just told Leo a trick to rid himself of that pesky hangover. Hang on a minute, Raven. Hey, Candy? Is everything okay?"

By this time, we'd made it across the cobblestone crosswalk. Candy's face was almost as white as the box she was carrying in her hands, though she tried to cover up her pallor with a half-smile. Those pesky little tingle sensations began to pierce my right palm.

"Of course, everything is fine," Candy responded immediately, attempting to cover up the fact that something clearly had her rattled. "Raven, happy birthday. I'm looking forward to the party at the pub tonight."

"Thank you, Candy. I—"

"Running late! Have a good day, and I'll see you later," Candy said in a rush, cutting of my question.

Liam and I both stood in shock as Candy continued to hurry down the sidewalk to her salon. I honestly wasn't sure how the donuts hadn't ended up face down on the street.

You're going to ruin my good mood, aren't you?

"How much do you want to bet that she saw the spirit of a loved one?" I whispered in dismay, the itch to search through the inventory at the antique store becoming quite unbearable. I should be at the tea shop with Beetle, organizing things for the big trick or treating event that began at six o'clock this evening. "We really need to find that object, Liam."

Have I ever told you that you're just about on par with Skippy when it comes to ruining my good moods? No? Well, you are. Good going, birthday girl. Good going.

Chapter Nine

"**L**YDIA, GOOD MORNING," Liam said after we'd walked into the antique shop. "How are you today?"

The quaint manner in which the old and delicate items were arranged on the vintage tables made a customer feel right at home. It was as if the family hearth had been lit, and the warmth spread throughout the room. Kathleen hadn't used the usual modern glass display cabinets, but instead opted to use various pieces of antique furniture that the patron could also purchase for their home or business. Among them were numerous curio cabinets to house the store's stock of knickknacks and collectable figurines. I'd often mulled over adding a few of the Queen Anne-style items to the tea shop, or maybe the early American seventeenth century William and Mary style tables she had closer to the built-in shelves along the wall. Of course, nearly all of the shop's inventory were late 1800 reproductions, but even they had tremendous value on the current market.

You should buy this nice oak rocking chair. It doesn't look pleasing to the eye in the least with this hideous shade of azure blue on the cushion, but it's very comfortable.

I cringed when I heard the slightest tug in the fabric from where I suspected Leo was sharpening his claws. The only reason Lydia couldn't hear the minor shredding was due to an old-fashioned granite birdbath that had the sound of calming running water splashing into a series of urns at its center.

"Liam, what a wonderful surprise," Lydia exclaimed, turning away from a table that she was arranging a display of tall white candlesticks on with the obvious care of a small business employee. "Have you heard anything new on Kathleen's case? She has a meeting with her attorney and the DA next week, and her lawyer believes there will be no charges filed against her. No one can say for sure until the DA says so."

I want to go on record saying that if you put something in my tea and I keel over from a previously unknown allergic reaction…I'll haunt you from the grave until you go completely insane.

Lydia had taken a brief pause after greeting Liam to tell me happy birthday, but her sole focus was unabashedly concentrated on him. Her appellant eyes sought a resolution that Liam didn't have in his power to reconcile. By this time, she'd made her way over to us with earnest to hear his reply. I remained silent while they chatted, giving time for Liam to work up to the reason we were here and using the opportunity to peruse the shop to make sure nothing else had been brought out from inventory in the days since I'd last visited the store.

"…have a request, if you'd be so inclined." Liam had finally finished the small talk and gotten to the reason we were here. "I was asked to check the local shops for an original antique object that has mysteriously gone missing in the not too distant past. Would you mind if I take a look at your inventory?"

"Of course," Lydia replied, grabbing a set of keys from the table in front of her. "You should know that we still have some items boxed up in the back, with the more expensive smaller ones locked in a safe."

That reminds me. We should get a pawprint safe for my premium organic catnip and my favorite Meerschaum pipe. You never know when Skippy might try to retaliate against my efforts to stop the squirrelpocalypse.

"Do you mind if I take a peek, too?" I asked, having already discussed with Liam how I could finagle my way into the inventory room with him. As for a safe for Leo's catnip stash, that wasn't going to happen. "I'd love to have first dibs on some of those items that you and Kathleen were able to get from that estate sale a few weeks ago."

You'll regret that decision when Skippy and his band of ninja misfits find a way into the tea shop, wreak havoc with all the china, and then scatter all the tea leaves in the wind. They're those kind of rogues...without honor.

"I'll let you join Liam in the back only if you don't tell anyone," Lydia said, shaking her finger in warning. "You know how Cora and the ladies from the auxiliary club are when it comes to exclusive previews of the items that we find at some of those estate sales. They hold special secret meetings for that exact purpose. It all makes for a very conspiratorial atmosphere. They thrive on it. I always sell at least half of the items that Kathleen and I cherry pick every time they ask to see some of the previously undisclosed inventory."

Not to sidetrack our current birthday scavenger hunt, but have you considered that Cora or one of her socialite disciples might have actually already bought the item in question?

Honestly, the thought hadn't even entered my mind. Leo had added on another layer of peril that now needed to be looked into, but he hadn't realized that only he would have the ability to make sure such an item hadn't already been purchased.

How do you figure that? And it better be good, because I have a squirrelpocalypse to stop in between these headache-inducing mysteries you keep stumbling over in a vain attempt to save this small village from obscurity.

One, I hadn't been the one to stumble over this particular mystery. That credit belonged to Leo, when he was the one who'd discovered all the occult items in the antique shop in the first place. Two, Leo was the one who had the ability to sneak into all their houses without being seen, all in the name of safety and justice.

I find your propensity to rationalize violating our neighbors' personal privacy quite disturbing, Raven.

"I promise not to tell a soul that you let me take a peek," I said, giving my pledge to Lydia that I wouldn't tell anyone about my little visit to the back room. Truthfully, the less anyone knew about it the better. "You're the reason my birthday is getting off to a great start, Lydia, so thank you."

It's too bad you can't just do a locator spell.

Leo and I had this conversation this morning, but it was quite difficult to cast an incantation such as that when we had no idea what we were looking for to begin with. My mother had suggested before heading to Beetle's last night that I tap into the energy level of the community. An object that could allow spirits to cross through the veil as if it were nothing more than thin air had to give off a moderate level of psychokinetic paranormal energy. It would cause a vibration in elemental forces that power the weave. The source of all arcane magic.

"Here you are," Lydia announced, flipping a light switch on the wall. The overhead lights instantly highlighted what could only be described as an antique treasure trove. If I hadn't set a financial budget, I could have very well ended up broke at the end of this tour. "Take a look around and let me know if you find anything you like, Raven. Liam, do I need to contact Kathleen about this missing artifact? Is there cause for concern?"

"No," Liam replied in reassurance, watching intently as Lydia unlocked a massive safe that could not be moved by a half-dozen humans, let alone us. "There's no need for immediate concern. I'm just doing a favor for someone, that's all."

Look, Raven. An antique scratching post. I wonder if it's better than the ones used today. I'll test it out to be sure.

I had to bite my lip to warn Leo that what he saw wasn't a scratching post, but instead an early American style oak coatrack. It was a good thing that the bell over the entrance chimed when someone had walked into the shop out front.

"Take as long as you need. I'll go and wait on my customer."

"Leo, don't you dare sharpen your claws on that," I whispered fiercely, batting at the air around the coatrack. "Start looking around for…"

Exactly. We have no idea what we're looking for, so do your thing with the energy. I've got parks to peruse and squirrels to chase. That home remedy the good ol' sheriff told me about needs to be packaged and sold in stores. We could make a mint.

"What are we looking for again?" Liam asked, having overheard my comments to Leo. "Remember, this is all new to me. I have no idea what a magical object is supposed to look like."

"Well, this is where it gets tricky," I said, cautiously glancing at the door that Lydia had walked through to the main part of the shop. The last thing I needed was for her to come back and find me doing a bit of magic. "It's not like witches can sense when other supernatural beings are around, and the same goes for magical objects. But if we tap into our inner abilities, I might be able to get the slightest hint of an object's energy, unless it is somehow cloaked. The more powerful an object is, the easier it should be able to detect. At least, in theory."

"So, it basically comes down to concentration," Liam said,

trying to sum up what I was attempting to do in layman's terms. "Alright then. This wasn't how I pictured spending part of your birthday, but there's nothing wrong with a little improvisation. Work your magic, Raven."

Actually, let's not be quite so hasty. No flubbed-up spells, Wonder Witch. Simply close your eyes, hone into the element powers around us, get a sense of...oh, never mind. That's just malarkey. Basically, relax and attune yourself with the energy flowing around you. Do it until you think you're going nuts, then you will begin to feel the hum of things around you.

I sighed in resignation, closing my eyes as instructed and doing my best to meditate. I was actually quite good at it after having taken a couple of classes in meditation when I lived in the city. It didn't take me long to even out my breathing, focusing my attention on draining all the tension from my body. Within a couple of minutes, my heartbeat was steady and I could even hear the faintest murmurs of conversation drifting from the main area of the shop.

There was a drone of quietness that came from being in a place filled with so much history, but nothing was giving off a wave of energy that might indicate that it was magical. I tried again, and then a third time, before utter defeat washed over me.

"It's not here," I said, not doing a very good job in keeping my desperation at bay. "Liam, what are we going to do? Tonight is All Hallows' Eve, when the veil is at its thinnest." I realized that the thickness of the curtain that hung between us and the afterlife wasn't the cause of the townsfolk encountering their long-lost loved ones, but it still worried me all the same. "You're the one who pointed out that we have no idea what we are looking for, and I don't have a spell for this."

"If we can just get through tonight without any major ghost

encounters that have the residents calling Ghostbusters, the veil returns to normal, right?" Liam asked, trying to put a positive spin on our failed search. He even rubbed my arm in comfort, but nothing was going to take away my uneasiness of having spirits visit their loved ones as if they were simply going on vacation. "Maybe we don't need to do anything but wait it out."

The palm of my right hand immediately warmed at the suggestion we do nothing.

Wait just half a witch's twitch. I might have a brilliant idea. You know, the good ol' sheriff's homemade remedy really starts the day off right.

"What idea, Leo?" I asked, not wanting him to get side-tracked quite yet. I was hesitant to even bring up the fact that he hadn't had a memory blip, as I liked to call it. "I'm at a loss here."

Hear me out, oh student of mine. I'm pretty sure I saw Skippy using the sandbox at the park to map out the best areas in town for his brothers to collect acorns.

I waited for Leo to reveal his brilliant plan, but he remained silent. I really, really needed to ask Liam about that home remedy for hangovers. It seemed to have given Leo a new lease on life, but I needed him to get back on good terms with the old lease. Skippy was probably using the sandbox as his own personal pantry to get through the upcoming winter months. Leo's brilliant plan was a few acorns shy of the ultimate squirrel trap blueprint.

It's not nice to be critical, Raven.

"Um, not to interrupt whatever it is that is happening right now," Liam muttered, rubbing the back of his neck in wariness, "but it's only a matter of time before Lydia comes back here to check on us."

"Leo, what does a sandbox and Skippy have to do with ghosts running around town?"

My nemesis keeps a list.

I waited for a more clearer picture, but Leo provided nothing. Now that I think about it, it was just like Leo to have paid a visit to the tea shop in order to ingest more edibles.

You're the one who seems to find it hard to follow my train of thought, Raven. We need a list of items that can attract spirits. Once we have that list and can narrow the objects down, we should then be able to cast a locator spell on each object. Mic drop! Is that a brilliant plan or what? You may now call me Professor Leo, Arcane Magister of the Mystical Arts.

I had to admit that Leo did have a great idea. One couldn't do a locator spell without knowing what item was being sought. Not to split hairs, but we usually needed something that belonged to whom we were attempting to locate, but this was an object. This type of locator spell was completely different than if we were searching for another person.

Genius, right? I know. I know. Speaking of knowing, that good ol' sheriff sure does know his stuff on hangovers, doesn't he? I feel good! So good. I feel good...da da da da da dat!

"Good job, Leo," I commended, not looking forward to when Leo had another crash. He was actually singing, and Leo never sang aloud. Of course, he was messing up the lyrics, but it was easy to distinguish the song. "Why don't you head back to the tea shop for your morning nap? I'll be there momentarily, and we can then work on that list together."

Leo was still humming as he walked toward the exit, disappearing from sight right before crossing over the threshold.

"Liam, you told him that old wives tale about hangovers, didn't you? The one where if you drink a little bit in the morning, it reduces the hangover symptoms? He went back over to the tea shop and ate some more edibles, didn't he?" I put my hands on my hips in disbelief as Liam's grin turned into a full-grown smile. "You realize that you only delayed the symptoms, right?"

"Hey, it works. That is, if you allow it to work by getting some rest and hydrating," Liam replied with a laugh, holding both hands up in defense. "I've been to my fair share of poker games. A Bloody Mary usually does the trick, but I wasn't sure that cats can drink that...so I resorted to the tried and true holistic remedy. Trust me, Leo's symptoms won't nearly be as bad as they were first thing this morning, given some time."

"Holistic remedy? Really?"

"Really," Liam answered boldly, following me out the door before I could disagree with him. "Trust me. Now, would you like to tell me about this list you're about to generate? Those one-sided conversations are really hard to keep up with."

Chapter Ten

I SPENT SOME of the morning decorating two of the high-top tables that I would use for the big trick or treat extravaganza tonight. One had a long, dark purple tablecloth with a black cat drinking tea while wearing a witch's hat. I'd also managed to stitch a string of orange lights around the bottom hem for an added effect. This particular table would be used for my spiced pumpkin samples of hot tea for the adults wanting a bit of a warmup while their children went shop to shop collecting mounds of sugar to rot their teeth.

Speaking of something sweet, I'd decorated the second table with a black cloth, white spider webs, and greenish glowing spiders for the candy display. I had a matching large porcelain bowl to hold all the sugary, sweet candies that the little ones would be craving this very night.

"Perfect, Raven! Just perfect," Beetle exclaimed after he'd reappeared from the back room. His habit of repeating words was very endearing. "You've outdone yourself."

I'd yet to set the tables outside, keeping them just inside the door for easy reach, but at least the trimming had been done. I had an outdoor outlet next to the entrance that I could use to power my tea kettle and the decorations on my tables. All I had left to do was to go home between closing and when trick or treating began in order to change into my witch's outfit, which freed me up to begin the list of known magical items that could possibly be responsible for the residents seeing their long-lost dead loved ones. I could then compare my list to an inventory of the items sold by the antique store over the past few months with the physical descriptions listed on the sales receipts.

"Thank you, Beetle."

I was pretty proud of myself for how the displays had turned out, usually not one to go too overboard. Being in a small town like this brought out a bit of a competitive domestic expression in me that I hadn't even known existed, and I was reveling in the close-knit community that I didn't have living in the big city.

Glancing at the big clock on the wall behind the counter, I realized that it was already going on eleven-thirty in the morning. Beetle continued to restock the seasonal flavors that were the biggest sellers today, not looking the least bit concerned that my mother had left the shop an hour ago and hadn't returned since.

"Where did Mom say she was going again?" I asked, hoping to trip up Beetle's answer. I began cleaning up the fabric glue and extra spiders that I could save for next year. "I was happy to hear that she's staying for my birthday celebration at the pub."

"Regina walked down to the bakery to pick us up some bear claws," Beetle said without hesitation. It was the exact excuse she'd given me when she'd left the shop, only she'd made a right out of the tea shop instead of strolling in the other direction. "Bree tried a new recipe last month, and she's outdone herself this time. Yes siree! She's outdone herself."

I'd been keeping a close eye on the sidewalk, and my mother had yet to reappear and begin her trek to the bakery in the right direction. For a brief moment, I worried that my mother might actually be the one responsible for the ghost sightings around town. Then I realized that she and Beetle had been whispering earlier with their heads together. I'd heard the word birthday and present, although not immediately together. Still, Mom must have slipped off to finish wrapping my gift, and that filled my heart with joy.

"Beetle, I'm going to go into the back room for a bit." I collected all the debris and extra decorations into the small box I'd confiscated earlier, and then began my way across the tea shop. It was time to finally solve a mystery. "I want to make sure I have Otis' holistic blend ready for him to pick up on Friday."

"I've got things covered, my dear Raven," Beetle said with a pat to his chest. "All covered."

It didn't take me long to slip through the ivory-colored fairy beads that hung on celestial strings that kept customers from seeing or hearing anything from the back room. It was technically a storage room slash working area where I created holistic tea blends with a sprinkle of magic to help those patrons who needed a bit of additional health benefits. I guess I never thought about it before, but I felt an inner peace back here that was strangely comfortable.

There is no inner peace to be had on a day like today, Raven. The squirrelpocalypse has begun. It's the beginning of the end. I've seen it with my own eyes.

It was a good thing I'd already set down the box on my worktable, because it freed me to put my hand over my mouth so that I could stop myself from laughing too hard and upsetting an already upset familiar.

This is no laughing matter, Raven. You're lucky you get to celebrate your birthday today, because we might not make it to mine.

"Leo, what in the world has happened?"

Similar to how Leo looked this morning with a bit of sway in his upper body, tufts of fur sticking out more than usual, and basically him looking like he'd been through a hurricane…let's just say he looked even a bit worse for wear now. There were bits and pieces of what looked to be food or maybe shells of some sort stuck to his fur.

Crushed acorns is what happened. It was open season, and the target just happened to be yours truly.

"Skippy and his friends caught you digging through the sandbox, didn't they?" I surmised, not able to contain my laughter any longer. "Please tell me that no one actually got hurt?"

An ordinary housecat might have done something regrettable, but Leo had more restraint. He'd never actually hurt another living thing. Well, my mother might be the exception, but he would only turn her into some form of reptile if he could ever find the missing spell from the family grimoire. I had a feeling that Nan had been the one to hide such a harmful incantation for the family's sake in general.

Those ninja squirrels are hard to take on when it's ten to one. I barely escaped with my life, and Skippy had a front row seat for the whole battle. Well, Operation Open Retaliation starts now.

"Operation Open Retaliation is going to have to wait," I reminded Leo as I grabbed a pen and pad from one of the shelves. I settled on the stool to finally figure out what kind of occult item could be hidden in one of the houses in town. "Go ahead and clean yourself off while we make this list."

Leo didn't appear particularly pleased with the delay of his next battle of wills, but he didn't fight me too hard on the change in plans. That alone told me that this latest mystery had him a teensy-weensy worried about the veil between us and the afterlife.

I'll give you five minutes to ruminate, and then I'm going to go see what kind of edibles that Beetle brought me this morning.

"Agreed," I said in approval, knowing that Leo would be able to list the items in under a minute. "I'm ready. I've already written down a crystal ball and a pentagram of some sort. Maybe a wooden one from a tree in Salem."

You've been watching too many horror movies.

I did notice that Leo didn't quite tell me that my thought process was out of line on the tree trunk theory. Wood had the ability to harness a lot of energy, so therefore anything made of a particular wood associated with witches would be able to summon spirits. At least, that's what I rationalized in my thoughts.

A wooden planchette, those pesky fairies, and a simple mirror for starters. Then there is a—

"A fairy?" I asked, thinking about Strifle. She was the familiar who we'd helped cross over to the other side so that she could be with Mazie Rose Young. "Can a fairy really harness enough power to cause spirits to return to our side?"

Those irritating glitter bombers can do a lot of things that would horrify you, Raven. I can't even bring myself to talk about the Feywild.

I had to wonder if Leo wasn't giving the fairies a little too much credit, but I wouldn't argue until I'd done more research on familiars. There was a lot to learn about the nuances of the supernatural, and I was reading up on it as fast as humanly possible while practicing my spellcasting.

"What about the mirror? You make it sound like any old mirror would do," I pointed out, uncomfortable with the idea that someone could simply look into a mirror and summon a spirit at random. "That's downright creepy, Leo."

I meant that a witch would be able to use a mirror if he or she had the right spell. If a mirror is being used as a portal and you aren't the one summoning a spirit, we might want to consider the resident warlock as the culprit. Let's face it, he's been out to ruin our perfectly happy lives here in Paramour Bay since day one.

"Rye took all your money at the poker game last night, didn't he?" I asked, chastising myself for not seeing where this conversation had been heading since Leo had agreed so quickly to clean off the acorn remnants of his earlier skirmish. "Leo, Rye has no reason to summon spirits and freak out the residents. Ivan isn't going to kick him out of his seat at the table because of a theory you've cooked up."

Whose side are you on, Raven? You'll have to pick one eventually.

"Let's get back to this list," I said, purposefully steering the conversation in the right direction. "We have six and a half hours to solve this mystery. Technically, six hours. I'd like at least thirty minutes to change into my costume without fearing the we're about to be invaded by a whole cemetery's worth of the afterlife."

Fine. Ruin my life, but you should know that it's your money I lost last night. I lost the whole household sundries fund, so you might want to reconsider my grand plan. Anyway, a Ouija board. And that's most likely the culprit after that stupid horror movie aired a few years ago.

Why hadn't I thought of a Ouija board? It made the most sense, there were quite a few teenagers in town who would absolutely think that it was nothing more than a mere game to be played with at slumber parties.

"Leo, you're a genius," I exclaimed with excitement, reaching for one of the local maps that Nan had stored on one of the shelves. I'd always wondered why she'd kept a stack of atlases, but it all made sense now. The majority of the crystals that I'd inherited from Nan were at home, but she had more of the common ones stored in a drawer here at the tea shop. "Liam is on a call, but I told him I'd touch base with him if we finally located the item in question. He said something about the Abbotts being upset about some kids wrapping the oak tree in their front yard in toilet paper."

Could have been Skippy and his ninja misfits. Come to think of it, I did see one of the minions running around with some toilet paper stuck to his back foot when I was ducking behind the slide.

It didn't take me long to lay out the map and light two candles, though I did make sure that Beetle was still content in the main area of the tea shop perusing the shop's account ledger. There was still no sign of my mother, but I had no idea where she needed to drive to in order to pick up my gift.

Oh, that reminds me…

I began prepping for the locator spell, waiting for Leo to finish his sentence. By the time I had everything ready, he still hadn't said a word.

"Leo? What were you going to say?"

I was saying something? Well, it couldn't have been very important.

I had been talking about someone TPing the Abbotts' front yard, although I'd been thinking about Beetle and my mother. Nine times out of ten, Leo's quip would have been about either Skippy and his merry band, my mother, or his supply of catnip. I was betting he'd been going to bring up something in regard to his edibles.

"Well, here goes nothing," I muttered, holding the amethyst on a string so that it hovered over the middle of the map. "*Close and near, never fear, the object I seek will appear.*"

I softly chanted the rhyming verse a few times to clear my head and harness energy from the elements around me. My mind cleared until I was able to focus solely on an image of a Ouija board that had been used to open a path to the other side. The amethyst began to gracefully rotate counterclockwise. With my other hand, I began to sprinkle some absinthe on the map. Within seconds, the dried pinch of the herb began to collect together as if they were magnetized iron particles. Unfortunately, they began to separate into three tiny dots as they each traveled to different areas on the map.

Hey, Raven. What are you doing over there? I'm a bit nauseated for some reason. I mean, not nearly enough to prevent me from eating my edibles today.

Leo was obviously still in the middle of his short-term memory blip. I remained silent, carrying on the spell a bit longer to confirm there were indeed three houses where I could find a Ouija board that had been active recently.

Ouija board? Wait just a snake's slither. Why are you...ohhhhh. Ohhhh, I just realized that the good ol' sheriff's home remedy for a hangover didn't quite do all its own magic. No pun intended.

"Do you feel better than you did this morning?" I asked, memorizing the residences where the absinthe covered them on the paper. It was a good thing this particular map was enlarged to the point I could make out the individual houses. "Please say yes, Leo, because we have to pay a visit to three people this afternoon to see if their Ouija boards are the reason spirits are popping up all over Paramour Bay."

I suppose, Leo begrudgingly admitted. *Can't you go gallivanting around town while I take a nap? Being the only one responsible for stopping this reoccurrence of squirrelpocalypse is utterly exhaust-*

ing.

"Then go eat your edibles so that you have enough energy to get through the day," I advised, not willing to let this spirit outbreak get out of hand before the trick or treating extravaganza. "It looks as if we need to pay a visit to Dee Fairuzo, Candy Hamilton, and…oh, wow."

Let me guess—Harry. Our local librarian was at the game last night, you know. Who would have thought a werewolf would have a need for a Ouija board?

"Not Harry," I corrected Leo, having mixed feelings about the third board. I mean, Dee and Candy's daughters having a game like that didn't surprise me in the least. But why in the world would an elderly woman in her nineties own a Ouija board? "It's Gertie. She has a Ouija board at the inn, Leo."

We are talking about the same crotchety old lady who can walk faster than me, conned your grandmother into teaching her a spell, and also stores pestles and mortars in her kitchen cabinets? Nothing to worry about there.

"We already ruled out the possibility of Gertie being a witch," I pointed out, carefully picking up the map on either side so that it was easier to slide the absinthe back into its container. "She does take a strong interest in the holistic. What if she's always just had a wish to be a…"

Go ahead. Say it. Our resident innkeeper has a wish to become a witch. There's no shame in rhyming, Raven, but don't you think it's a little late in life to be wanting to switch up careers?

I quickly folded the map and slid it between the others on the shelf. Once the amethyst was stored away in the drawer, I quickly checked Otis' order for Friday. I'd worked on some of the so-called holistic blends earlier this week in anticipation of the All Hallows' Eve preparations and the time they would take.

"I'm ready," I announced determinedly, pushing the stool back a bit so that I could stand with ease. "Let's solve this mystery, Leo."

Ease up there, birthday witch. My edibles are essential to my mental health, especially with the lingering side effects from this monumental hangover. Snacks over mysteries, Raven, and I'm not going anywhere without having my proper nourishment first.

Chapter Eleven

"LEO LOOKS AS if he has a skip to his step," Liam said as we both walked down the sidewalk. The crisp air had a slight bite to it now that the coastal breeze was coming in off the bay, but it didn't seem to bother Leo in the least. He was walking in front of us, deciding that maybe Gertie would give him some extra treats like she was prone to do with some of the other cats around town. "I take it he's still feeling somewhat better than this morning?"

"He complained a little bit about nausea after I'd cast the locator spell, but Beetle's edibles seem to have provided a remedy for that problem," I replied wryly. I couldn't help but closely study those residents whom we passed on the street for any sign of distress. The scuttlebutt around town hadn't indicated anyone other than Candy getting a glimpse of a long-lost loved one recently. "Eileen seems to have rationalized the entire ghost situation."

When I'd called Liam to explain about the three Ouija boards, he had just been finishing up with the Abbotts. I'd told him my idea about speaking with Dee and Candy with the ruse of *borrowing* a Ouija board for tonight's party. Of course, we had to pretend that we didn't know that their daughters even owned one, but the excuse had been valid enough. We would conveniently forget to bring them with us this evening, but at least it would give me an opportunity to see if the boards held any residual energy.

"Trust me, sometimes it's easier to find any excuse to hold onto rather than accept that there are unknown forces at play in our everyday lives." Liam winked, having been sheriff in a town with a resident witch for a very long time without being any the wiser. "I have been meaning to ask you something."

No. It is much easier if he doesn't know anything he could repeat in the wrong company.

Leo had shouted from up ahead, having turned his left side toward me so that I couldn't miss his disapproval. He only included his justification after seeing my facial expression.

No hand in marriage. Not happening. Your mother doesn't even know that the good ol' sheriff has been brought into the inner circle. Can you imagine if…

Leo came to a complete stop, interrupting whatever it was that Liam might have wanted to ask me. As a matter of fact, tufts of Leo's fur were standing on end as if he'd just found out that the neighborhood squirrels had won in the battle of wills.

Didn't the resident warlock say that the Wicked Witch of Windsor was in town?

"Keep moving," Liam murmured encouragingly, lifting his hand in acknowledgement as Newt drove by in Otis' vehicle. He'd complained about a rattling sound in the engine well before I'd moved to Paramour Bay, and I'd come to the realization that he took it in once a month to see if Newt could miraculously discover the reason why. "What's wrong, Raven?"

"Apparently, Aunt Rowena is in town. Rye stopped into the shop yesterday. He dropped that bombshell on us, saying she was having her house renovated this week and that she'd decided to stay with him until her renovations were complete." I did agree that it was odd not have seen hide nor hair of the woman. "We haven't seen her at all, and that has Leo worried."

In my experience, that evil sorceress doesn't do anything without a reason. She never would have stepped foot inside the town limits when my beloved Rosemary was alive.

We were just about to cross the intersection to where the inn sat on the corner lot when my mother appeared out of nowhere. All four of Leo's paws came off the sidewalk in surprise, but that was nothing compared to the adrenaline spike in my bloodstream.

"Mother!" I exclaimed, but her eyes had already widened in what could only be described as alarm. She quickly composed herself, even lifting a hand to pat the back of her hair. She pretty much always wore her hair in an elegant swoop off her neck, held in place with a decorative clip and a few bobby pins. "What are you doing? More importantly, where are you coming from?"

Why are you asking these questions when the answers are so obvious, Raven? Regina Lattice Marigold, confess! You're having an illicit affair with Ivan, aren't you? How could you betray my BFF?

I wasn't even going to try to figure out how Leo had connected those ridiculous different-sized dots.

"I was simply taking a walk," my mother responded with poise, completely ignoring Leo. She usually wasn't one to let quips like that go, but I almost forgot that she had no idea that Liam knew of our family secret. I had no choice but to follow her lead or give away the fact that I'd broken the same coven rule twice. "Liam, aren't you looking handsome today."

"It's good to see you, Ms. Marigold," Liam replied, stepping forward and allowing my mother to kiss his cheek in greeting. "It is a beautiful day for a walk, isn't it?"

The good ol' sheriff isn't buying that load of squirrel pellets, is he?

I would have stepped on Leo's tail to stop him from saying anything else had my mother not continued to carry on her conversation with Liam, thankfully not thinking through the meaning behind Leo's words. On the other hand, usually nothing got past my mother.

"I might have also been planning something for my daughter's birthday celebration this evening," my mother said with a sly grin thrown Liam's way.

Don't think you can throw me off your trail, Regina.

"Liam, why don't you go ahead over to the inn," I suggested, hoping that he would understand why I needed to speak with my mother in private. "I just want to speak with Mom for a moment. I don't want Gertie to be left waiting for us."

I would have to make up some excuse about seeing Gertie on business, which wasn't a stretch. Gertie bought all of her tea blends that she served at the inn from me. I could say that Liam was just spending as much time as he could with me since it was my birthday.

"Mom, you promised me that you weren't the reason there are spirits roaming around Paramour Bay," I whispered in dismay to her once Liam had walked on across the cobblestone intersection. "You were coming from the cemetery, weren't you? Did a spell go wrong? Did you inadvertently say the wrong thing and—"

"Raven, don't be so paranoid," my mother chided, her green eyes darkening with disappointment. "I have done nothing of the sort, and I'm hurt that you would even think I would dabble in the craft haphazardly. You know very well I don't practice on a regular basis, with the exception of helping you out of a bind here or there.'

Don't fall for it, Raven. She's the queen of manipulation.

"I'm not talking to you, feline ingrate."

Then my day is made, Regina.

"Would the two of you just stop?" My temples were beginning to throb, and my blood pressure was definitely elevated. The palm of my right hand still contained a few piercing tingles, but they'd technically been there since Wilma had told me about Merle's spirit paying her a visit. "Mom, please tell me the truth. What are you doing on this end of town?"

It was true that my mother had moved from Paramour Bay thirty-one years ago, claiming that she had wanted a fresh start without any magic involved. For thirty years, I had no idea that I'd come from a family of witches. Once the cat was out of the bag, so to speak, I'd realized that my mother hadn't truly given up the craft. There had been times that she'd utilized magic throughout my childhood, and the fact that she hadn't lost her magical touch told me that it had probably been more often than I thought.

"If you must know, I paid a visit to Heidi about tonight's party regarding my gift to you. If you'd like to ruin your birthday surprise, I can certainly continue and spill the beans this minute. I daresay, Raven, I'm disappointed that you don't trust your own mother."

Ouch.

I glared at Leo, especially since he had been the first one to jump to conclusions.

I'm not her daughter, so don't go smearing your guilt onto my back. Besides, I was just protecting my BFF. We can't have your mother breaking his heart into a million pieces.

"I'm sorry," I said with a sigh of resignation. "It was wrong of me to jump to conclusions. It's just that you've been gone from the tea shop for quite a while, and Beetle mentioned that you were going to the bakery to buy some bear claws or some such story."

For all that my BFF does for the good people…and familiar…of this town, he deserves more than a few bear claws. Seeing as I don't have to live up to your standards as a daughter, I'm going to go on record that I don't believe a word of this malarkey. I might have memory lapses here and there, but I do recall how your mother acted when she was trying to pull the wool over my beloved Rosemary's eyes.

"Oh, that was just an excuse so that you didn't know what I was up to for your birthday," my mother explained with a dismissive wave of her hand. "Leo, no one ever pulled the wool over my mother's eyes. Just like Raven can't do it to me."

Ohhhhh, snap!

"There is no snapping to be done, Leo," I argued, still not giving my mother the satisfaction of confessing to something that she might or might not be aware of. She might think there was something fishy going on with me, but she couldn't prove it. Leo fumbling at the goal line wasn't going to happen, either. "I've been upfront this entire time about the residents seeing the spirits of their loved ones. The only thing I haven't mentioned is that Aunt Rowena is in town."

"Why on earth would Aunt Rowena be in town?" my mother asked in shock. At least, I hoped that she hadn't known about Aunt Rowena being in Paramour Bay this entire time. The hand over her chest was just the right touch of disbelief. "If you knew all this time that she was here, why would you assume that I had something to do with the spirit visits instead of her? Really, Raven, I'm disappointed in you."

Why do mothers always use that phrase on their children? It's a wonder you turned out as well as you did. I'm not saying that you're completely free of her influence, but you're not totally messed up, either. Wait. Who am I kidding? You're a complete mess.

I agreed with Leo that the disappointment speech could leave a mark, but maturity and gaining a bit of wisdom made me realize that it was just a method used to get me to do things her way instead of mine. Well, that wasn't going to happen today.

"So, you haven't seen Aunt Rowena while you've been galli-vanting around town?" I asked warily, watching my mother's expression very closely for any sign that she was lying. "Rye said she's been staying with him, but I highly doubt that she's staying inside of his house this time of year."

You know, it makes me wonder if that isn't why your mother glued those fake spiders to her eyes. You know, so you can't tell when she's lying like a rug.

"I haven't seen Aunt Rowena gallivanting around town," my mother replied with a dainty sniff. "Besides, she isn't one to gallivant. Now isn't the time to get into the family drama, but she has been doing her best to make amends this past year."

"Are you suggesting…" I couldn't bring myself to finish my sentence. Mom was right. Now certainly wasn't the time to delve into the fact that Aunt Rowena had chosen the coven over her own sister. Not to mention that she'd purposefully cut that same sister out of her life until it had been too late to make amends. Or the fact that she was now a leader of a faction that wanted complete control over the coven's governing council. "I have to wrangle some spirits, and you have to return to the tea shop with some bear claws. I'll see you this afternoon."

This is it, isn't it? Leo asked, scampering a step ahead of me as we crossed the cobblestone intersection while my mother walked in the opposite direction. *The squirrelpocalypse has already happened, otherwise I wouldn't have heard that blasphemy come out of your mother's mouth. Was she seriously suggesting that we absolve the Wicked Witch of Windsor? Maybe we should take shelter. I know for a fact that those crushed acorn shells sting like a mad hornet.*

"I'm not sure what that discussion was all about, only that we weren't finishing it in the middle of town," I muttered while attempting to shake off the feeling that something wasn't quite right with the run-in that had just taken place. "Remind me to check in with Heidi after we finish collecting the last Ouija board. I think it's best we confirm that Mom actually went to Heidi's office today."

It didn't take Leo and I long to walk up the grand front steps of the inn, taking a moment that we technically didn't have to admire the Halloween decorations. Rye helped out Gertie a lot around the inn, doing odd jobs here and there to keep the exterior looking as splendid as it had back in its day. There were cornstalks, jack o'lanterns, and strings of orange lights strategically outlining the porch in precision. It was the singing skeletons on either side of the pillars that had the neighbors coming out in droves to watch the show. The extraordinary nighttime entertainment was something to behold every Halloween season.

I opened the door, inhaling that sweet fragrance I'd come to associate with the inn when I caught sight of Liam looking a bit pale. He'd actually been employed by the NYPD before returning to Paramour Bay to take over as sheriff after Otis had retired. On top of that experience, he'd handled my confession better than anyone would have in that situation. Come to think of it, I'm not sure I'd ever seen him disconcerted before.

You know what? I've decided that my time should be better

spent monitoring your mother's odd behavior of late. Gertie's treats are usually of the generic kind, and you know those types of nibbles always give me heartburn. I'll just be on my way.

"Not so fast," I muttered, leaning down and scooping him up in my arms. That was no easy feat, considering his heft. I wouldn't have stood a chance of nabbing him had he been invisible. "Liam? Why is Gertie dancing around the dining room table?"

First your mother's need to make amends with the Wicked Witch of Windsor, and now a ninety-year-old woman is practically skipping through her house like Mary Poppins on catnip. What do you think happened, Raven? The squirrelpocalypse, that's what!

"Gertie saw her high school crush today," Liam murmured, running a hand over his face in disbelief. "Wallace Nickelbaum."

"Let me guess," I whispered, glancing around the large main floor of the inn to make sure there were no guests lingering about. Leo tried to finagle his way out of my arms, but that wasn't going to happen. "Mr. Nickelbaum has been dead for quite some time."

"You could say that. Gertie is fixing us tea, in case you wanted to know why she's practically twirling around the dining room table without her cane." Liam cleared his throat, causing Gertie to wave at me before she went into the kitchen. "What did your mother have to say?"

"Mom tried to convince me that she went to see Heidi this morning about my birthday present. She then proceeded to suggest that we should make amends with Aunt Rowena, which has Leo and I a bit on edge."

That's it! I figured it out, Raven.

Leo had stopped wiggling, his left eye widening with realization about something I hadn't quite connected the dots to since we'd spoken with my mother. My arms were beginning to hurt from holding him this long, and I eventually had no choice but to set him down gently on the beautiful hardwood floor.

"What did you figure out?" I murmured, watching closely for Gertie to sail back into the dining room.

The Wicked Witch of Windsor has teamed up with Skippy and his minions. It makes perfect sense. I don't know why I didn't figure it out before. Two of my most infamous nemeses working together to conspire against me.

"Here we are," Gertie announced, returning to her favorite chair at the dining room table. Beverly, who worked part-time at the inn, followed closely behind carrying a tea tray with all the fixings in the inn's finest china. "Isn't today just beautiful? We couldn't have asked for better weather for tonight's trick or treating event. Leo, come here, you handsome thing."

Well, seeing as I wouldn't want any treats to go to waste before the world crashes down around us...

Leo scampered across the hardwood floor, onto the ornate oriental rug, and began nibbling on the morsels of food that Gertie had set down in a small pile. Her arthritis still seemed to be under control as she went about putting sugar cubes into her teacup.

"I hear it's someone's birthday," Gertie exclaimed in glee, motioning for me and Liam to join her at the dining room table. "I'm so glad the two of you stopped in to pay me a visit."

"We were actually hoping for a favor," Liam said with a smile, diving head first into the request we'd come to make. He'd recovered quickly and most likely because Mr. Nickelbaum wasn't still hanging around. At least, I didn't believe he was still here at the inn. I wasn't about to ask, either. "You wouldn't happen to have a Ouija board, would you? I'm throwing a small get-together for Raven's birthday at the pub this evening. Given the holiday, I thought it would be fun to have some games set up on the tables. I know you keep some games on hand for the young guests, so I thought there was a chance you might have a Ouija board in that mix."

"Oh, I do wish you'd stopped in earlier this week," Gertie replied with a frown. She gently set the teaspoon on the saucer with the faintest delicate click. "I gave that silly old board game to Rye this past Monday."

Leo practically choked on one of the morsels he must have inhaled after his gasp of horror, while I was just grateful that I hadn't taken a sip of my tea. It would have undoubtedly been spit out over the gorgeous lace tablecloth.

"Rye?" Liam repeated, seemingly as surprised by this outcome as we were. "That's an odd request. Did he say why he would want a child's game?"

Liam understood that even though the box was marketed for eight years and older, a Ouija board wasn't a game to be used for simple entertainment. With that said, he was still trying to keep up appearances. I gave him a lot of credit for not stumbling.

Heartburn. I'm going to die of heartburn, and it's all that flipping warlock's fault.

"You know, I don't believe I asked him outright. I'd just assumed that he was going to use it for a decoration or some such thing," Gertie replied, carefully lifting her teacup to her thin lips. Her hands trembled a bit, but she was surprisingly steady for a ninety-year-old woman. "Would you care for some coffee cake?"

Liam was nice enough to continue to carry on the conversation while I thought over this latest development. Had Rye just borrowed the Ouija board for some type of Halloween decoration? It was more than likely that he'd borrowed it for some nefarious reason, though why he wouldn't have simply gone to a store to buy one without leaving a trail was beyond me. Why had he been so blatant about borrowing a magical item when he was a warlock? Rye was an intelligent man, so maybe there was some measure of legitimacy to the reason he gave Gertie.

I hate to break this to you, Raven, but Rye cheats at poker. Anyone who cheats at poker doesn't have legitimate reasons to borrow a Ouija board. I mean, are you forgetting what happened earlier this summer? He thought that he was to blame for that empty crypt in the cemetery after conducting a séance to speak with his ancestors. The next logical step when that didn't work would be to use a Ouija board. Oh, my heartburn might catch my fur on fire. Is that a thing?

"…thank you for the tea, Gertie. Will you be able to stop by the party later tonight? I bet you could give us a run for our money on the dance floor."

"Oh, Liam, you are good for my aging heart," Gertie said, laughing heartily as she sat back in her chair. "I'll get my enjoyment by handing out candy to the little ones this evening, and then I'll be taking these old bones to bed and reading a bit of Edgar Allen Poe to finish out my night."

As we exchanged goodbyes, I couldn't help but wonder if Leo was right about Rye wanting the Ouija board to contact his ancestors. He'd been adopted as an infant, and then practically lived on the streets as a young boy when he began to show signs that he was different. It wasn't until Aunt Rowena caught sight of him using magic in an alleyway that he finally had someone to look out for him.

Are you trying to make me feel bad for our local warlock? It won't work, Raven. Ivan, Ted, and Harry didn't notice, but I witnessed Rye Dolgiram's cheating with my own eyes. He was dealing seconds. If he wasn't burning cards between the turns, I'd bet that catnip farm in Alaska that he was dealing seconds at Texas Hold 'em.

Leo didn't own a catnip farm in Alaska. Besides, it wasn't right to bet on something that could have serious consequences for the town. A part of me could actually relate to Rye wanting to discover where he came from and who his biological family was, because I'd spent a lot of time asking Leo questions about ours.

Right, right. I don't own a catnip farm in Alaska. I don't know what I was thinking. Actually, I wasn't thinking. I probably had a memory blip, like you're always calling it. Yeah, that's it. By the way, ignore that voicemail on the home phone from that commercial realtor. Solicitors and all that. Can't live with them, can't set them on fire.

"What's the plan?" Liam asked once we'd walked back down the porch steps. "You and I both agree that no one should be aware that I have knowledge of the supernatural. I don't think it's the best idea to go with you to talk to Rye."

"First, I think it's safe to say we found the object in question that has been allowing the spirits to come and go as they please," I said in reassurance, grateful that I wouldn't have to locate some other rare artifact. Almost everything was pointing toward Rye and the Ouija board he'd confiscated from Gertie. "You're right, though. I also know that you wanted to check in with all the shop owners to make sure they were set for tonight. You go and take care of that while I go have a chat with Rye. Whatever he may have done to the veil, the two of us will be able to fix, especially with Aunt Rowena's help."

I forgot about the Wicked Witch of Windsor. You know, this heartburn is only getting worse. I know you love me and wouldn't want to see my fur catch fire, so I'll just head on back to the tea shop and make sure that your mother isn't mistreating my BFF. I wish you the best of luck, my dear Raven. Witchspeed.

Chapter Twelve

*Y*OU WOULD HAVE *felt really bad making me come with you had my fur caught on fire from my heartburn. Why did you let me eat those treats after I specifically told you that they give me heartburn? You know that old biddy only buys generic kitty treats.*

"You know that, too," I countered, not taking blame for Leo's uncontrollable eating habits. "You're just lucky that those nibbles didn't contain the red dye that you're allergic to."

We were standing outside Rye's two-story house that was located in the back of one of the older neighborhoods. I'd opted to drive instead of walk, just in case I found out that he was on a jobsite and I had to track him down. Either way, at least I'd get a chance to speak with Aunt Rowena while I was here.

Don't change the subject, Raven. Did you know that there wasn't any red dye in those treats? Or did you let me eat them without knowing, waiting for my face to explode as I swelled up like a baboon? That's attempted murder, you know. I hold you totally accountable.

"Oh, would you stop being so dramatic," I chastised, walking up the thin walkway to a beautifully crafted porch that was void of any Halloween decorations whatsoever. Rye was one of the few who hadn't gotten into the spirit of the holiday. I guess being a bachelor gave him a pass in the eyes of the residents. Me? I knew for a fact that he was a warlock, so the least he could have done was carve a pumpkin or something traditional. "If Aunt Rowena doesn't answer the door, you might need to pop on inside and take a look around to see if the Ouija board is laying out in plain sight."

And risk the chance of finding the Wicked Witch of Windsor dancing naked around a cauldron of boiling children? I don't think so, Raven. Right this minute, I could be back at the tea shop eating my favorite premium edibles and spending time with my BFF. This was not how we were supposed to spend this year's All Hallows' Eve.

"I'm in complete agreement on that sentiment." I gingerly walked onto the newly-built porch, wondering how much Rye would charge me if I were to add a screened-in version of this onto the back of the cottage. The design really was beautiful, and his craftsmanship was superb, bar none. "Unfortunately, it falls on our shoulders to keep this town spirit-free."

Why does the resident warlock get a pass in that burden? Or our local werewolf, for that matter? And we're forgetting my good friend, Ivan. I don't mean to throw him under the bus, sickle and all, but he's only doing half the job. I wonder if his boss knows how slipshod his work has gotten.

I rang the doorbell, listening closely for any sign of life behind the front door.

"Do you think that this Ouija board is the object that's causing the spirits to come and go as they please?" I whispered, still trying to decipher if anyone was walking around inside. "I mean, what if it's something else and we're just wasting time? I'd say this could be postponed until tomorrow, but tonight at midnight is when the weave is at its strongest."

I rang the doorbell again before looking over my shoulder to see if anyone was around. The leaves had begun falling to the ground earlier this month, painting the yards with my favorite autumn colors. A light breeze carried a few of the dried leaves across the driveway, which was when I made note that Aunt Rowena's vehicle wasn't parked in the street.

"Leo, you need to—"

No. I'm beginning to wonder if that particular word was left out of your personal dictionary.

"Aunt Rowena isn't here, unless she parked her car inside the garage," I said, trying to reason with Leo. "Come on. Just go and take a quick peek inside the living room to see if the Ouija board is in there."

Don't we already know that the ghost-summoning contraption is inside? Just call the resident warlock on your phone and demand that he hand it over. Bust him and don't let up. At least one of us can feel satisfied.

I walked over to the window, presumably the one that gave a view into the living room. The curtains blocked most of the interior, leaving me even more frustrated at Leo for making this situation difficult.

"Leo, all you have to do is—"

"What on earth are the two of you doing snooping around here?"

At the unexpected sound of my mother's voice, Leo completely panicked and disappeared, leaving orange and black strands of fur floating in his wake. I was no better, spinning around from the window and cracking my elbow against the wooden frame. With my hand over my heart, I somehow managed to hold back my scream of alarm.

"Mom! Why would you sneak up on us like that?"

"I think the better question is why are you sneaking around and looking in Rye's window? How would you feel if he drove out to the cottage and was sneaking around like some peeping

Tom?"

Don't answer that, Raven. She's trying to get you to admit to being a peeping Tomette. And just for the record, I didn't panic. I simply did as you asked and took a look around the resident warlock's living room. See? No overreaction here. You really should stop projecting your fears onto others, Raven.

"Rye has a Ouija board, and I think he's the reason why spirits have been roaming around town," I blurted out, not able to come up with any believable excuse as to why Leo and I did look like peeping Toms. "Rye has been trying to contact his ancestors, and he might have succeeded a little too well."

Way to go, Raven. Where is Heidi when we need her?

Heidi was definitely a better liar than me, by a landslide. Unfortunately, she was still at work. She didn't have the luxury of taking time off during the middle of the day to go ghost hunting.

"Honey, what on earth would make you think that Aunt Rowena would ever allow such a thing to happen?" my mother asked, expertly putting a hole in my theory. She certainly had a way of making me doubt myself. Leo had been spot on when he said she was a master manipulator, though she wasn't a bad person. It was just her nature. "Wasn't that the very reason Aunt Rowena had Rye leave the coven in the first place? On top of that, she definitely wouldn't have allowed him to use such a device to summon spirits right before All Hallows' Eve."

I hate to admit this, but your mother does have a point. Maybe that's why the Ouija board isn't here, because the resident warlock doesn't want the Wicked Witch of Windsor to know that he's been moonlighting as a medium.

"Mom, what are you doing here?" I asked skeptically, watching her closely for any sign of deceit.

You could stare at your mother until the cows come home, but she's a pro when it comes to the art of the con. You'd think that Ivan wouldn't want that type of person at his poker table, but we are talking about my good friend who can't tell when a warlock is counting cards. Hey, you don't think our local grim reaper is defective, do you?

"I became curious as to why Aunt Rowena would have renovations done on her house on the exact week of All Hallows' Eve," my mother reluctantly admitted, finally displaying her distrust of our aunt. "I figured I'd pay her a quick visit to gauge the situation. Now that you told me about Rye, I'm wondering if that isn't why she's here."

In a weird way, that actually makes sense. That alone makes me skeptical. I really don't like it when your mother has a good explanation for things, because it never turns out well.

I remained silent for a moment, taking the time to consider my mother's theory. It did make sense, but there was a tiny hitch in her assumption.

"Gertie saw her old high school flame earlier today," I revealed, unsettled that the residents hadn't connected the dots. Although, Elsie had convinced Wilma that Merle's spirit had been nothing more than a figment of her imagination. Eugene thought he was just getting old and senile. I'm not sure about Candy, but Gertie might actually truly believe that she'd seen Mr. Nickelbaum. "If Aunt Rowena did come here to stop Rye from contacting his ancestors, I'm not so sure she succeeded in that endeavor."

"Has Leo bothered to share with you that our powers become stronger on All Hallows' Eve because the veil becomes somewhat blurred between the living and the dead? It allows our ancestors the ability to help us should we have need of their powers."

I'm relatively sure your resident helicopter mother just insulted my teaching abilities. Now you listen here, you MILK—Mother I'd Like to Kill, in case you were wondering about the acronym.

"Yes, I know all about the history of All Hallows' Eve," I replied wryly, trying to avert another argument between the two. Besides, I might have just figured out what had gone wrong with the cleanup. "If Rye had used the Ouija board earlier this week in an attempt to take advantage of the thinning veil while curtailing a massive fallout, would Aunt Rowena even be strong enough to basically hold back the entirety of the afterlife?"

My mother seemed to ponder my question. I hadn't even considered that maybe the reason Aunt Rowena hadn't stopped by the tea shop was due to her trying to rectify Rye's mistake. With that said, Rye certainly hadn't seemed as if he'd unleashed the afterlife during our conversation yesterday morning.

The resident warlock deals seconds, Raven. I wouldn't put anything past his poker face.

"I'll take one for the team," my mother said matter-of-factly, digging inside her purse for her phone. "One call should clear this up."

I wasn't aware that your mother was a part of our team. Did I miss the memo? I'd like to abdicate my position. Do you require a two-week notice?

"Stop that," I admonished, grateful that my mother was willing to handle the Aunt Rowena part of this problem. "We're going to need to find out where Rye is this afternoon if Mom can't get ahold of Aunt Rowena."

Is it possible to receive a hall pass for abject job dissatisfaction?

I purposefully didn't reply to Leo, not wanting him to think he could skate on this spirit invasion crackdown. Thinking back over what we'd discovered these last two days, Mom's theory made sense that Aunt Rowena had found out about Rye's wanting to use this devout holiday of the supernatural to summon his ancestors in order to find out where he'd come from and why he'd been abandoned at such a young age. That type of magic was like a human's Black Friday right after Thanksgiving. I couldn't imagine any spirit wanting to miss an opportunity to speak to a loved one on this side of the veil. No wonder Ivan hadn't wanted to get involved. It must have sounded like a stampede as they all tried to fit through the so-called curtain.

Mom had stepped off the porch to place the call to Aunt Rowena, and her expression as she made her way back up the handcrafted steps told me that she was about to deliver some bad news. She was already dropping her cell phone back into her purse.

"Aunt Rowena isn't answering my call."

Hopefully, she had an appointment with Ivan...you know the kind I'm referring to.

"That's fine," I said, having already accepted that today wasn't going my way. "I'll go find Rye, and then we'll get to the bottom of this. Whatever he's done in attempting to reach out to his ancestors in hopes of finding out who his biological parents are, it can be corrected."

My mother arched that eyebrow of hers at the perfect angle.

"Don't give me that look, Mom," I said in warning, pulling my cell phone out of my skirt pocket. If Rye didn't answer, then I'd simply have to drive around town until I saw his truck. "You were the one who always said that any mistake made could be corrected if you went about it the right way."

And you actually listened to her? Heaven forbid! Raven, I'm beginning to understand where everything went wrong. We're not taking her with us, right? I call shotgun!

Chapter Thirteen

I SHOULD HAVE known that Rye wouldn't have been that easy to track down. First, he wasn't answering his phone. Secondly, he was nowhere to be found around town. A part of me had a sneaking suspicion that maybe he'd actually managed to carry out a successful séance and had been able to speak with his ancestors. Had Rye finally located his biological parents? Had Aunt Rowena been trying to stop him or was she helping him? I wasn't sure about a lot of things, but it was becoming clearer and clearer that the veil between us and the afterlife had basically become an open window.

"...something in the coffee," Cora said to Desmond as the couple walked past the open door of the tea shop. "I mean, it's a good thing I didn't have a hair appointment today. I overheard Maude say that the poor woman had a tremor in her hand all day. Speaking of Maude, did you know that she swears she saw her dead brother? I'm telling you, it's as if someone put drugs in..."

I glanced over my shoulder to see my mother roll her eyes at Cora's assumption that there was something in the coffee or the water over at the diner that was making the residents of Paramour Bay see their deceased loved ones.

Not to perplex you further, but don't you find it odd that my beloved Rosemary hasn't paid us a visit? Let's not forget Mazie or

Lucille. It would also be nice to get ahold of that irritating gnat of a fairy to find out how to take this glitter bomb off my paw.

Beetle was standing right next to me as we finished positioning one of the high-top tables right outside the tea shop's door. I did my best not to show a response to Leo's question. I guess I hadn't put too much thought into it, but Leo had a point. Why *hadn't* Nan stopped by to visit if the veil had been pierced or parted?

"Raven, dear, you better get home to change into your costume," my mother urged as she began to open the bags of candy that I'd be handing out to the children in about an hour. "I'll keep trying to reach Aunt Rowena. It's quite possible that she and Rye drove up to Windsor to check out those renovations of hers."

I'm no longer offering up my catnip farm in Alaska. I've decided it's too valuable, but I'd like to go on record that I don't believe for a moment that the Wicked Witch of Windsor nor our resident warlock left town. They're up to no good and may be using the holiday to focus their powers somehow.

I completely agreed with Leo, but it wasn't like I could say anything in front of Beetle. My mother hadn't left his side since I'd returned to the store, so I'd had to rely on Leo to get my point across several times. Needless to say, Leo wasn't as diplomatic as I would have been.

Look, your mother already has a golden ticket for the express train to Hades. There's no reason to sugarcoat anything anymore.

My mother pasted a smile to her face with those painted red lips of hers, probably doing her best to bite her tongue, thereby preventing herself from giving Leo a scathing reply. Leo's needling for the past couple of hours was wearing on her nerves.

I'm stuck here with you until this entire ghost invasion is taken care of instead of making sure that the squirrelpocalypse doesn't commence, so I deserve something to keep my mind off the end of the world.

"Delicious," Beetle exclaimed, having snuck one of the candy bars from the bowl my mother had filled with various types of treats. "Simply delicious! That reminds me…"

Beetle patted his cardigan sweater where the pocket of his dress shirt was located directly beneath the fabric. He began walking over to the display window, causing the strands of his white hair to sway with every step.

"Here you go, my friend," Beetle crooned, slipping his fingers inside his sweater to pull out a small foil packet of premium organic catnip. Leo had been sunning himself on his cat bed with his paws up in the air while we waited for Rye to call back, but he scampered as quickly as he could into an upright position. "It's Halloween, and everyone deserves extra treats today."

I love him, Raven. I just love him so much.

"You're up to something," I murmured, having taken advantage of Beetle's distraction to speak with Mom. "I can tell, so you better spit it out now."

"I have no idea what you're talking about," my mother replied haughtily, moving the wrapped treats around in the bowl as if she were rearranging flowers inside a vase. "You saw me try to call Aunt Rowena. She wasn't answering, so just how is it that you believe I'm up to something, dear?"

"Maybe because you called Ted after Beetle told you about the unexpected ghost visitors," I pointed out, connecting the dots that there was more to this supernatural event than met the eye. "Ted dislikes you, Mom. You know that, so why would you call him if it wasn't to garner information and use it to your benefit?"

You two are making it very hard to enjoy my delicious treat. My taste buds deserve to savor this tasty edible gift from the gods. Your bickering sours my stomach.

My mother's smile grew as Beetle made his way back to us, but I'm pretty sure her happiness had to do with the fact that she couldn't answer me without him overhearing. I had no choice but to let her off the hook for now.

"I'm going to drive home and change into my costume," I announced, having every intention of stopping by the cemetery to visit Ivan. He'd mentioned that I'd find my answers close to home, which we did in the form of a Ouija board that I still couldn't locate. To top off my worry with a bit of added stress, we were basing everything on the so-called game as being the object in question. What if there was another artifact in town that was calling forth these spirits? "I shouldn't be too long. I'll be back before the trick or treaters begin to arrive."

"We'll hold down the fort, my dear Raven," Beetle said with a puffed-up chest and a smear of chocolate on his bottom lip. "No worries here. No worries at all."

My mother's eyes narrowed as she studied me after realizing that it shouldn't take me an hour to change into my costume. Well, she'd have to be the one to wonder what I was up to for once. Leo and I had places to be and grim reapers to see.

It's a good thing that my BFF gave me an extra serving of my favorite blend of kitty herb.

"Thanks, Beetle," I called out over my shoulder, not giving my mother a chance to figure out a way to stop me. "And don't eat all the candy! It's meant for the children."

I quickly made my way out the tea shop and to my car, knowing that Leo would do his blipping thing. Sure enough, by the time I'd settled myself behind the steering wheel, Leo was sitting in the passenger seat, licking his whiskers.

Why are we visiting my good friend at the cemetery? Notice that I didn't say BFF. I only have room for one of those, and that slot is reserved for my supplier.

"Ivan knows more than he's letting on," I replied, having been pondering the grim reaper's cryptic message since last night. "He said that the answer was close to home."

Well, that was true. I mean, our resident warlock did take a Ouija board from the cheap old biddy who won't buy any treats that aren't generic Chinese imports.

I turned the key in the ignition, bringing the engine to life in my old clunker. Leo always referred to my beat-up old Corolla as a deathtrap, but she'd been good to me for many years. Had I not been running out of time, I would have feigned turning at the cobblestone intersection in order to be heading back toward my cottage. Instead, I continued to drive down another block and turn left onto the one street that would take me directly to the cemetery.

"For some reason, I don't believe that Ivan meant the Ouija board." I was finally able to share my doubts with Leo now that my mother wasn't picking up every word Leo thought in his head. "Did you see the way Mom laid her hand on Ivan's arm? Who purposefully touches a grim reaper?"

I do agree that it was a foolish gesture, but you seem to forget that we are talking about your mother. There are times that I think the woman truly believes she's invincible. Oh, the grief she used to cause my beloved Rosemary. I can't seem to recall a specific moment, though.

Great. Just what I needed before seeking out Ivan—Leo's memory going on the fritz.

You know my edibles help me in that area, Raven. Oh, ye of little faith. Two squirrels plus two more squirrels equals a squirrel-pocalypse. See? Spot on.

"Thinking back to last night, the palm of my hand became slightly warmer when Mom reached out to touch Ivan. You don't think that she would be stupid enough to try to use magic on him, do you?"

Is that why we just pulled up to the wrought-iron gate of the cemetery? I know our local grim reaper personally, Raven, and I can attest that he would have escorted your mother right through the veil if she'd done anything so…idiotic. That's the only adjective I could come up with for something so reckless.

I did agree with Leo's assessment, but what if Ivan didn't remember Mom using some type of spell on him?

I don't think you're asking yourself the right questions, Raven. If you believe that Regina wanted to influence Ivan, I would be asking why. You're basically suggesting that she is the one responsible our current ghost invasion.

"I know," I replied quietly, having shifted my car into park.

I scanned the cemetery, but I couldn't find a single soul.

Seriously? A single soul? Does a grim reaper even have a soul? You know those types of befuddlements confuse me.

"I don't have an answer as to why Mom would want to…" I let my voice trail off as something clicked, but I couldn't accept that my mother would go so far as to put the welfare of the good people of this town at risk. "Leo, you don't think Mom would open the floodgates of the afterlife just to force me out of Paramour Bay, do you? It's been exactly one year since I inherited the tea shop, which according to Nan's will means that I could legally sell it and the cottage to make a profit."

This is one of those times that you want me to lie, right? I get confused as to what you want me to answer sometimes.

Mom had always tried to get me to move back to the city, but she hadn't really mentioned it in quite a while. I had to be off-base, right? I mean, she wasn't so greedy as to think I'd actually sell everything I had here just to move back to the city, was she? Paramour Bay had become my home. These residents were like my family. Not to mention Leo, who was my mentor, confidant, and partner in crime. Ted had become a...well, like that wise uncle who everyone went to for advice. I mean, my best friend had moved here to join me in this blissful, slower way of life, and I'd finally met someone I was falling madly and hopelessly in love with each passing day. My mother would have to take these precious gifts I'd been given from my cold, dead hands.

Really? We've discovered that we have a local grim reaper stationed at our very own cemetery, and you go and say something like that? Oy vey. It's like I've got to pull your head out of the lion's mouth on a daily basis.

"Come on," I encouraged, now even more determined to find out what was going on in this town. Ivan knew more than he was telling, and even I could see the importance of putting a cork into whatever hole had been opened for spirits to roam about willy-nilly. "Let's go look for Ivan. We have one hour before the trick or treating event begins, and the last thing we need are real ghosts crashing our Halloween party."

In case you didn't notice, it's a little late for that. On the plus side, those extra treats that Beetle supplied me with has put a little skip into my step. It helps that I'm now good friends with the local grim reaper, and this will give me a chance to see what dish I'm supposed to bring to next week's game. It rotates. Besides, I want this ghost invasion stopped as much as you do. I finally have my seat, and I'm not about to let some pesky ghosts get in the way of our next game.

Chapter Fourteen

"THIS ENTIRE DAY has been one failure after another, Heidi," I complained, using a third bobby pin to secure my witch's hat into place. I loved the wide purple band that matched my dress. I took one final look into the bathroom mirror to ensure myself that the glittery, matching eyeshadow hadn't been smeared and that I hadn't smudged my plum lipstick. I shut off the overhead light as I walked out into the hallway. "What if more spirits make their way through? The veil is already a bit thin this time of year, and now it's as if someone installed a revolving door in it. How in the world can I keep this under wraps?"

What's worse than an expulsion from a coven? Is there one? I'll need to give it some serious thought. I'd tell you not to worry about supernatural prison, but I've heard whispers about such a place. There is one, and it's not for the faint of heart.

"Leo, you better be giving Raven a pep talk," Heidi said from her place next to one of the stools at the counter. She was using the second rung to zip up a white knee-high boot. "Ivan wasn't at the cemetery. Is that so odd? I mean, he was probably out collecting souls. That is his job, after all."

Heidi set her foot down and blinked those baby blue eyes of hers a few times in incredulity.

"I said that so callously," Heidi exclaimed in disbelief. Her pink lips formed the perfect O. "If Ivan was out doing his job, that means people died. That's horrible. What's even worse is that we don't even know how far his area of responsibility extends. What if it was someone right here in town?"

That's a great question. I'll have to put that on my list of topics to cover when I'm trying to distract Ivan from a good hand.

"Just because Ivan wasn't at the cemetery doesn't mean that he was out greeting newly departed souls," I said, wincing at the way I'd described an escort into the afterlife. "I'm hoping that he decided the veil needed to be mended before midnight and went to fix it. Either that, or he talked to someone who could."

"It's downright creepy to think of how things like that work, and I'm already on edge that I could see my dead grandmother appear in front of me with a disappointed look at the costume I chose for tonight. It's cute, right? Not over the top?"

Heidi had opted to go as a fairy, much to Leo's dismay. He wasn't even in his bed near the front window. As a matter of fact, a quick look around the living room told me that he'd opted to go the invisible route. He'd probably stay that way, all but guaranteeing that Heidi couldn't wrestle him to the ground to put him in a unicorn costume.

The wings on the back of her white, silver, and pink outfit were the centerpiece, but I personally loved the elaborate fabric that was layered with sheer sparkly material that give Heidi an ethereal appearance. I would bet dollars to catnip that the unicorn costume matched her outfit.

I'm not taking that bet. My catnip is too precious to be used for such sacrilege.

"You look beautiful," I told Heidi sincerely, pulling out my phone to see if I'd received a message from Rye that I'd some-how missed. Considering I'd left him ten voicemails and had been checking my phone religiously, it was highly doubtful that I'd overlooked a response. Still, I couldn't help myself. "I'll meet you at the shop. I want to see if either he or Aunt Rowena went home at some point, purposefully ignoring my calls. I wouldn't put it past Aunt Rowena, but I thought Rye was better than that."

The doorbell rang, but it couldn't have been Liam. I'd spoken to him a bit ago, and he was overseeing the trick or treating event to make sure that main street was blocked off for the children and their parents to roam freely. He'd already set up the large orange cones and detour signs, but it wasn't that hard to navigate the side roads of Paramour Bay.

It must be the giant grey Crayola. Don't answer the door. The last time that wax for brains rang the doorbell, he was accompanied by the Mistress of the Darkness Below. I had a nightmare about her last night. Not pleasant.

I carefully made my way to the front door, making sure that the hem of my skirt didn't get caught in the heel of my shoe. What greeted me actually had me speechless, although Heidi squealed in joy and clapped her hands together.

I wonder if Ivan has another golden ticket for that express train to Hades. What I think of this sight in front of us is definitely enough to send me there.

"Ted! I love it!" Heidi exclaimed, quickly making her way to where Ted had stopped just inside the door enough for me to shut it behind him. "And you even have a trickle of red down your chin like blood. That is face paint, right?"

Ted stood there wearing one of his usual black suits, although he'd put on a black cape with one of those high necks like an old-fashioned vampire. His teeth were chipped and crooked all the way around, so he hadn't had the need for plastic fangs.

The only other adornment besides the cape was the trickle of fake blood down the right side of his chin. The fact that Heidi had cautiously asked if the coloring was from face paint would have made me laugh had I not also contemplated for a nanosecond that it might be real.

"The red coloring is from a berry, Miss Heidi."

"I like that you're cutting loose tonight, Ted," Heidi said, holding her hand up so that Ted would give her a high five. He stared at the palm of her hand for a moment before tilting his head just so in a bit of confusion. "Slap my hand. It's called a high five."

Ted did as instructed, though I wondered if it wasn't time to bring that mannequin to life to provide him some company. Maybe I could somehow add into the animation spell an inherent ability to blend in with society. It would do Ted good to have some sort of social guide. I'd have to look more into it, though, because messing up a spell like that could have dire consequences.

Give it ten years. Okay, maybe twenty. Either way, Ted deserves a few more poker games to hang with the guys.

"Ted, you're going to drive into town with Heidi," I advised, noticing that Leo was still invisible. He wasn't chancing Heidi getting ahold of him to put him in that adorable unicorn costume. "I'm stopping by Rye's place to see if he or Aunt Rowena are home. They borrowed a Ouija board from Gertie, and we think that maybe Rye was using it to contact his ancestors."

"Oh, you won't find Miss Rowena at Mr. Rye's house."

I caught myself waiting for Ted to expand on his declaration. Heidi did the same, and I wondered if we'd ever get used to Ted's short and concise replies. He only ever answered the question asked, and nothing more. Now that I think about it, Ivan had been the exact way last night, though he was more fluent in speaking his thoughts.

Neither one is that articulate when it comes to table talk during the game. Rye and I pretty much carry the conversation. You know, now that I think about it, not one thought crossed our resident warlock's mind when it came to the Ouija board and talking to his ancestors.

"That would have helped to know, Leo," I said with exasperation. I focused on Ted, already knowing I needed to ask the right question in order to get an informative reply. "Ted, do you know where Aunt Rowena is right this second?"

That was a little bit too direct, Raven.

"Yes."

See?

One would think that Heidi could hear Leo's quips with the way she bit her bottom lip to keep from laughing.

"Where is Aunt Rowena, Ted?"

"At the cemetery."

Well, I didn't see that one coming. Wait just a toad's wart. Do you think that's why we couldn't locate Ivan this afternoon? Sweet angel of mercy! The Wicked Witch of Windsor kidnapped our very own grim reaper!

Chapter Fifteen

"**L**EO, WE DON'T know for a fact that Aunt Rowena had anything to do with why Ivan wasn't at the cemetery this afternoon."

Even as I said those words, a part of me was extremely suspicious that very thing had happened without anyone being the wiser. With that said, didn't a grim reaper have a lot more arcane power than an ordinary witch?

Did you just call the Wicked Witch of Windsor an ordinary witch? What is wrong with you? Have you gone into a sugar coma?

"Ted, what was Aunt Rowena doing at the cemetery?" I asked, hoping that the reason had to do with something nicer than kidnapping Ivan…like visiting my Nan's grave to ask for forgiveness. "Did you talk to her?"

One, that first question was too open-ended for our stick of wax to contemplate. Two, you know you can't follow up with a second question or you'll just get the one answer. It only confuses him. Get with the program, Raven.

"I did not speak with her, Miss Raven."

"Could you see what Aunt Rowena was doing?"

"No."

"Was Aunt Rowena near Nan's tombstone?"

"No."

"Did Aunt Rowena—"

"Ted," Heidi exclaimed, waving both of her hands to stop me from peppering Ted with so many questions. "What were *you* doing at the cemetery?"

I was getting whiplash there for a second. Thanks, Heidi.

"I was helping Mr. Ivan repair a door on the Whitley family crypt."

Oops. Our fault, but no one needs to know anything about that Carry on.

"What time was that?" I asked, knowing full well that Leo and I had walked all the way back to the line of crypts that were pretty much reserved for the founding families. There had been no one in sight. "Leo and I were at the cemetery earlier this afternoon."

"I'd say an hour ago, Miss Raven."

That explains it. At least we know that my good friend wasn't skirting his duties.

"In what part of the cemetery did you see Aunt Rowena?"

That was very specific. Look at you go, Raven. It only took you a year, but there's nothing wrong with being a slow learner. Unless that was a one-off.

"Near the Watson family crypt," Ted replied, his frown deepening as he finally caught on to the fact that Aunt Rowena was probably up to no good.

Heidi and I shared a look of dismay. This wasn't good at all, and we might have a very big problem on our hands. Gertie belonged to the Watson family. There was clearly a connection between the Ouija board and Aunt Rowena, and that connection was Rye. With that said, I was no longer sure if Rye had wanted the Ouija board for himself.

But why would Aunt Rowena want to let spirits invade Paramour Bay?

I'm confused again. One minute, you think your mother had something to do with this ghost invasion. Then you changed your mind, believing that our local grim reaper was sleeping on the job before later deciding that Rye simply wanted to talk to his ancestors. You've now moved onto the Wicked Witch of Windsor as your prime suspect. You know, I'm not so certain that my headache this morning was from last night's overindulgence in catnip. I'm leaning toward my hangover being caused by trying to keep up with your logic.

"I'm reevaluating this mystery as the evidence develops moment to moment," I explained, feeling more confident about this latest theory than the other ones. I mean, Ted had seen Aunt Rowena with his own eyes near the Watson family crypt. There was one more question that would solidify my belief that she was the reason the residents of Paramour Bay were having visits from those beyond the grave. "Ted, was Aunt Rowena carrying anything with her?"

"I do believe that Miss Rowena was carrying a very large tote bag."

We're headed to the cemetery, aren't we? I'm fine with that, honestly. No unicorn costume for me. I mean, seriously. I think it's very sweet that my beloved Heidi wanted to accessorize me to go with her costume, but there are some lines that shouldn't be crossed. You can tell her. I'll meet you there. If we're going to deal with the Wicked Witch of Windsor, then I need to call in a few reinforcements.

"Why would your aunt want to lower the veil?" Heidi asked, not waiting for my answer as her she walked back to the counter where she'd left her purse. It was made from the white shimmery fabric that matched her wings, which were fluttering with each step she took. "Ted, you have a choice. I can drop you off to help with the trick or treating event, or you can come with us to the cemetery. I don't think it's wise to let Raven go deal with Rowena herself. Besides, Rowena will be extra careful with a human around."

I adore my beloved Heidi's optimism. She has no idea the lengths the Wicked Witch of Windsor will go to get her way, which is apparently to Hades and back on the express train sitting beside your mother.

"How are the preparations coming along?" my mother called out after throwing the front door open. We all startled at once, with even Ted putting his hand over his heart. Mom came to an abrupt halt when she saw all of us gathered round, with the exception of Leo. He was still invisible, and he would likely stay that way until Heidi lost interest in stuffing his rather haggard but portly body into a unicorn costume. "I can see we're all dressed, but why the long faces? It's All Hallows' Eve, as well as your birthday, Raven. This is time for celebration, unless..."

My mother narrowed her emerald green eyes in Heidi's direction, whose own eyes widened as if she'd been caught with her hand in the cookie jar. The sight was enough to cause Leo to abruptly appear standing on his pillow, a few strands of his fur still floating in the air.

Why does my beloved look so guilty, Raven? I've never seen that expression before. It's like she's been caught aiding and abetting my nemesis in the squirrelpocalypse. Where's my pipe? I feel an anxiety attack coming on.

"Unless what?" I asked hesitantly, not sure who to focus on first. Heidi had a will of stone, but my mother was as hard as a bedrock. "Heidi, what's going on?"

Doom and gloom is what's going on by the look of it. I feel an asthma attack coming on, Raven. Your mother has somehow convinced Heidi to go over to the dark side, and I don't know what to do with that kind of revelation.

Heidi had a sudden and intense interest in those sparkly, shimmery things on the fabric of her clutch purse. I'd thought she'd been awfully quiet as she'd gotten dressed into her costume, but I'd just assumed that the fairy wings had been giving her a bit of trouble. Now, I realized that she'd been attempting to sail under the radar.

"Your mother was just concerned that I told you about the birthday gift she got you," Heidi hedged, though I could tell that she was telling me the truth by the way she met my gaze. Unfortunately, I still witnessed a bit of guilt in her baby blues. "We should head to the cemetery, don't you think? We don't have all night."

Oh, whatever this birthday gift is…it's bad. I mean, really bad if my beloved Heidi would rather spend an evening with the local grim reaper than let it slip to you whatever it is your mother bought you. The suspense is killing me. Who did she murder?

I was more afraid that the birthday gift itself might be the reason we ended up being escorted by Ivan to the other side, but it was Aunt Rowena who was currently holding that proverbial door open while using the Ouija board as a doorstop.

You're right. It's better to be kept in the dark. Heidi didn't spill your secret, Regina. So tell us why you're here, because I'm almost certain that it wasn't to change out of that Mistress of the Dark outfit.

"Why are all of you going to the cemetery?" my mother asked, completely ignoring Leo as she focused on me. "Raven, it's your birthday. The children are about to start their trick or treating stroll down River Bay, stopping at all the small shops that have gone out of their way to make this All Hallows' Eve a success. You don't want to miss that, do you?"

I didn't answer my mother, but instead focused on Ted. He was staring at my mother with suspicion, and I immediately recalled running into her when Liam and I had paid Gertie a visit. She'd acted very similar to how Heidi had a few moments ago.

Don't go insulting my beloved Heidi by comparing her to your mother. That's like comparing sunshine to mud stuck to the bottom of your shoe.

"Heidi, did my mother stop by your office today?" I asked, cutting off my mother's sarcastic retort to Leo.

"Um, maybe?" Heidi offered, shooting daggers in my mother's direction. "I was quite busy today. Did you stop by the office, Ms. M?"

I was all for presents, especially the kind that were well thought-out and personalized. I'd foolishly assumed that my mother's gift fell into that category, but I was quickly changing my mind. Whatever my mother had gotten me was enough to cause Heidi to believe I wouldn't be thrilled upon opening it.

Then don't. Problem solved. Now, let's go fix the other issue at hand so that I'm not torn between stopping a ghost invasion or preventing a squirrelpocalypse. I'm only one familiar, and I can only do so much with the amount of catnip I've ingested today.

"The problem isn't solved, Leo." I put my hands on my hips, planting my boots firmly on the hardwood floor. "Mom? Spill it. Now."

Heidi took a slow and deliberate step back. Had my apprehension not reached the highest point possible, I would have laughed when Ted mimicked her movement.

"Fine. Ruin the surprise," my mother exclaimed, throwing her hands up in the air. "Beetle and I are getting married."

Leo gasped, promptly choking on something he must have

swallowed.

"We were going to formally announce our engagement at your birthday party."

A lot of thoughts were bouncing around in my head, and I was definitely wishing I'd taken Leo's advice about ignoring the problem at hand. We still had to seek out Aunt Rowena in order to stop this so-called ghost invasion she'd inadvertently let take over Paramour Bay. Plus, I'm pretty sure Leo had gone into a full-blown asthma attack from the wheezing I heard coming from his cat bed. I could relate, because I was at a total loss for words.

"Uh, Raven?" Heidi called out to me, tilting her head as she scratched her neck. I'm pretty sure she'd broken out in hives, and her clarification of the situation pretty much confirmed it. "In case you haven't connected the dots, that means your mother is moving back to Paramour Bay to be near all of us. She made me promise not to tell you, and the consequences of doing so were quite dire."

I'm almost certain the thud I heard was Leo's body hitting the ground after he'd stopped breathing from hearing such an announcement. On the bright side, the ghost invasion wasn't sounding so bad in comparison…mud and sunshine.

Chapter Sixteen

"**I** CAN'T BELIEVE you didn't tell me about my mother moving back to town," I scolded Heidi as we parked in front of the cemetery. I was still in shock by my mother's announcement. "I mean, this is a monumental decision that affects all our lives."

Affects our lives? Be honest, Raven. It's over. We'll never be at peace again. There's no need for an express train to Hades when the fiery pit has been brought to us by way of broomstick.

We'd had to take the side roads since Liam had already blocked off River Bay. I could already see the children and their parents lining up for the costume parade prior to the big event, but there was a really good chance that I wouldn't be a part of this year's tradition.

"I was going to tell you before we left the house," Heidi said defensively, wrestling with her wings as she tried to shift in her seat to get a better look at me. She grabbed ahold of my hand. "You've been so happy, especially after sharing your secret with Liam. I just wanted you to be able to spend the majority of your birthday without worrying about your mother moving back here. I didn't expect her to show up out of the blue when she was supposed to be helping Beetle get ready for the little ones to come marching down the main drag for their candy."

You realize there's not enough catnip in this backwater part of the world for me to handle your mother on a daily basis, right? I'll need daily injections. Sweet angel of mercy, she's turned me into a junkie, and she hasn't even moved back here yet!

"Mom got concerned that you were going to spill the beans," I said to Heidi, having already figured out why my mother had left Beetle to his own devices. I also understood why she was currently parked behind me, with Ted in her passenger seat. He hadn't been too pleased that he'd had to ride with her, but Heidi had needed the extra room in my vehicle for those wings of hers. "Which you would have done, and I should have recognized that something was bothering you sooner. You were quiet, and I'd just assumed it was because Jack couldn't be here for some of the festivities."

Some of the shops along River Bay had opted to have a few additional activities, such as bobbing for apples and haunted mini-houses. I hadn't had time to create something so extravagant. I was definitely going to do something next year, because I categorically refused to allow another ghost invasion to ruin my birthday.

Does this mean we can have the Wicked Witch of Windsor thrown into jail for the foreseeable future? I'm sure she'd like company, so I'll come up with some reason for the good ol' sheriff to arrest your mother, as well.

"No one is being arrested," I countered, opening my car door. I'd had to bend my witch's hat just so in order to keep it on top of my head. "Leo, just show yourself. We have too much going on for Heidi to try and wrestle you to the ground attempting to put that unicorn costume on you."

"I'd pay to see that," my mother retorted as she came to stand next to me. I found myself staring at her, wondering what I was going to do with her living so close. Once again, I found myself actually thinking that a ghost invasion didn't come close to competing with my mother's announcement. "Now, Ted managed to clue me in on everything that's taken place in the last few hours. It sounds as if Aunt Rowena is helping Rye contact his ancestors, although I have no idea why she would do such a thing. I mean, it's one of the reasons that she sent him away from the coven to begin with."

I wonder where Ivan keeps his appointment book. Do we know any forgers, Raven? We can slip your mother's name in one of the open slots and write it off as a business expense.

"Listen here, you—"

"Both of you just stop," I warned the two of them. The instant headache I'd gotten upon my mother's announcement began to pound even harder in my temples. "We're here to make sure that the residents of Paramour Bay are safe, thereby keeping our secret and the supernatural realm safeguarded from harm. Ted, why don't you lead the way back to the Watson family crypt?"

Ted's cape lifted a bit in the slight breeze as he quickly by-passed the crooked wrought-iron gate of the cemetery. Had anyone been about to witness his entrance, they would have been certain they'd seen a real-life vampire with their very own eyes. Add in a fairy and a witch with a cat, and it was definitely a Halloween card in the making.

I shot a warning glance at Leo when he would have made a comment about my mother being Mistress of the Dark. He'd finally decided to show himself, and he was currently attempting to walk gracefully alongside Heidi while he maintained a safe distance from Mom.

"Do you feel that?" my mother inquired cautiously, falling into step beside me. It was very rare that we presented a united front, usually because she was constantly lecturing me about living my life as a witch. "There's a low hum of supernatural current in the air."

Don't fall for that false sense of security, Raven. Your mother is up to something, and now I'm going to be forced to split my time between the squirrelpocalypse and the momageddon. It's not going to be pretty. Many lives will be lost, but the greater good will prevail.

Dusk had already fallen, allowing those low patches of fog to begin inching their way through the graveyard. The haze was practically hugging the tombstones, yet some were distinctly clear. Ted was methodically moving forward in his usual manner, so I didn't get to catch a glimpse of the names engraved into the sandstone.

"You'd think we'd be used to this by now," Heidi whispered as she walked to my right, grabbing my sleeve to make sure we were inseparable. "Yet I still think a hand is going to burst through the grass and grab ahold of my ankle."

My beloved Heidi is usually so careful when it comes to jinxing the situation. We haven't had to deal with zombies yet, and I'd like to keep it that way. Tell her to hush. I don't want to have to trip her, Raven.

"I'd be more worried about a flying apparition trying to possess your body," my mother countered matter-of-factly, without even the slightest trace of fear. "Raven, you didn't answer me. Do you feel that muted current of energy?"

First zombies, now possession. Have we learned nothing this past year? You two are insufferable.

I certainly did detect what my mother was referring to, but I didn't want to admit it out loud. Leo was right about the entire jinxing thing. We'd done it one too many times. Besides, the subdued sensation was getting stronger the closer we got to the back of the graveyard. I'm pretty sure even Heidi and Ted could feel the change in the air by now.

The caw of a black crow came from up ahead. I didn't miss the fact that Leo instinctively disappeared, only to reappear without missing a step. I hadn't noticed it before, but the crisp air was actually becoming quite colder the farther we advanced toward the crypts.

I have no idea what you're talking about, Raven. You blinked. Nothing else happened.

"Good evening."

Heidi and I both let out a short-lived squeal upon hearing Ivan greet us from the dark shadows of a lone tree that was in the process of losing all its leaves. Even my mother let out a small gasp and rested her hand over her heart, though she pretended to then brush off some imaginary lint. Ted was the only one who seemed unfazed by Ivan's sudden appearance. Leo was simply nowhere to be found.

"I see that you're here to pay your aunt a visit again," Ivan said to my mother as he balanced a shovel in his right hand. It was a rather creepy vision, but I was too stuck on the fact that he'd all but confessed that my mother had been here before. "I was about to go have a word with her myself, but I can see you brought reinforcements this time."

Wait just a skeleton's knee bone, did my good friend just say that your mother has been here looking for the Wicked Witch of Windsor before tonight? Regina Lattice Marigold, have you switched back to the dark side?

My mother gave an uneasy laugh as she shifted her weight and avoided my stare. Heidi was encouraging me to stay calm, but that was hard to do when my hurt and anger began to merge into a ball of heat in my hand.

"It's not what it sounds like, Raven." My mother shook her finger at Ivan, as if he were the one responsible for her actions. "And no, Leo, I haven't switched sides at all. I just didn't want your birthday to be ruined, Raven, so I tried to handle Aunt Rowena on my own. Unfortunately, you know how she gets when she sets her mind to something."

"Mom!" I exclaimed in total disbelief, feeling somewhat relieved that my mother had categorically denied any previous involvement in our current ghost invasion predicament. "You can't keep things like this from me. I've been running around for two days trying to figure out what was going on, and you knew the truth this entire time."

That's right, Raven. Don't let your mother off the hook. As a matter of fact, I'll drive the boat and we'll drop her body somewhere out to sea.

"In my defense, I only just figured everything out this afternoon."

"Isn't that when you ran into your mother?" Heidi murmured, still casting a suspicious glance Ivan's way. He and Ted were now standing side by side, watching my mother and I argue about her terrible decision making and lack of judgement. "She only dropped by my office for a few minutes, and it sounds like she was gone from the tea shop much longer than that."

"Heidi, dear, I'm right here," my mother scolded, clearing her throat before she straightened her shoulders. I recognized that stance, and she was getting ready to go to battle to defend her actions. "Raven, it's simple. I'm in love."

What in fiery Hades does that have to do with anything? Raven, don't let her wiggle her way out of this like some lost puppy stuck in a fence. I saw one of those before, you know. It's a ploy. Next thing I knew, I was side by side with Skippy helping the poor thing loose.

What did I get for my trouble? Slobber. It's in their DNA.

"You do realize that this town has been inundated with spirits of the residents' dead relatives, right? You're the one always saying that humans can't know about the supernatural, and yet you just sat back and allowed Aunt Rowena to open the floodgates," I exclaimed, unable to comprehend how my mother thought that she'd done the right thing in the name of love. I wasn't even sure what love had anything to do with it. "Wilma, Eugene, Gertie, Candy, and countless others have had encounters with spirits. They're eventually going to figure out that those ghosts might very well be the real deal."

Keep up the good work, Raven. You're on a roll. Don't cave now!

"What I'm trying to say is that I'm in love with Beetle," my mother admitted, still holding her own and refusing to acknowledge that she shouldn't have tried to handle anything on her own, especially when it came to Aunt Rowena. "I realize that my moving back to Paramour Bay after thirty-one years is a major decision for all of us, and I knew that it would come as a shock to you. I wanted very much for you to be okay with me getting married, as well as me being around more often. When I figured out that Aunt Rowena might be the guilty party that was basically unleashing the afterlife, I thought the additional stress might be a tad bit too much. I paid her a visit, believing that was all that was needed to end whatever it was she was trying to accomplish this All Hallows' Eve."

Guilt Trip 101. Don't fall for it, Raven. She's clearly at the top of her class in this subject, and we haven't had time to prep for a debate. I say let the energy balls fly!

"You should have told us the truth, Ms. M." Heidi twisted her pink lips in disappointment. "Let's face it. Ghosts aren't something to mess with. I know that, and I'm only a human. So, the chances of a possession are higher with me here than the rest of you. I'm feeling a bit hurt that you threw me under the bus like that."

Tell Heidi that if she's not careful, your mother will hop in the driver's seat and run her over until she's nothing but a pile a glitter. Great. Now I'm having horrible flashbacks. Asthma attack incoming. Why is your mother still alive? A shallow grave will suffice.

"Wait a second." We were all standing around arguing about the fact that Mom had kept something from us, but that something was still taking place in the Watson family crypt. "Mom, you make it sound as if this is all Aunt Rowena's fault. Isn't she simply helping Rye contact his ancestors?"

I sense a sudden U-turn coming up in this conversation. Run away! Run away! I get carsick, even on a bus.

"Not exactly," my mother said hesitantly, clearly not wanting to ruin what was left of my birthday. That moment had come and gone as fast as Leo could disappear. "You know, darling, it's still not too late for you and Heidi to head back to the tea shop. You can—"

"I suggest you all work together," Ivan advised, twirling the shovel in his hand as it balanced by the handle on the ground. "I do have an appointment to keep in approximately three minutes and twenty-one seconds."

"I do admire your work ethic," Ted said with a small nod of respect as if we weren't standing in the middle of a cemetery attempting to prevent more spirits from crossing over.

Speaking of appointments, do you use a planner, Mr. Ivan?

"That appointment isn't in our town, is it?" Heidi asked cautiously, keeping her blue eyes trained on Ivan for any hint of who might be the next individual to be escorted through the veil. "What exactly is your area of coverage, if you don't mind me asking?"

"Leo can find that out later," I muttered, wanting more than anything for my mother to fess up what she knew about Rye. "Mom?"

I'm not sure I'm ready to hear the answer to your question yet, Raven. I haven't had a hit off my catnip pipe or a nibble of an edible in over an hour. One must prepare for news like this, you know.

"Fine," my mother said, finally relenting when it was clear that no one in our little group was leaving the cemetery without fixing this mess once and for all. "The governing council of the coven is no longer in existence. The two factions have completely splintered, and Aunt Rowena is now leading the opposition. She thought help from our ancestors would aid her in battle, but that's not exactly going as intended. There was a slight hiccup in her plan of action."

"Hiccup?"

Sweet angel of mercy, what are you doing, Raven? I know from experience that hiccups aren't good. We don't want any part of Rowena's hiccups, so let's take your mother's first suggestion and go back to the tea shop. My BFF has edibles to help ease our anxiety. I'm sure they even have cures for the hiccups, so it's a two for one, and you know that I don't share with just anyone. If I were you, I'd take me up on my offer. Yes? Yes! Heigh-ho, heigh-ho, it's back to the car we go...

Chapter Seventeen

"WE AREN'T GOING anywhere, Leo," I exclaimed, setting my hands on my hips so that my mother knew I meant business. "Mom, what kind of hiccup did Aunt Rowena get herself involved with?"

I'm going to have to start carrying some edibles around with me, aren't I? Raven, remind me to buy one of those over the shoulder bags with an outer pocket. I'll pay you back after next week's poker game.

"Oh, it's nothing really," my mother tried to downplay, even waving my concern off as if the residents hadn't encountered any ghosts in the last two days. "Let's just say that your grandmother and the rest of our ancestors want no part in this war. They have, what you might say, gone on strike in the afterlife."

Scratch the "paying back" promise. I'm considering that satchel part of my mental health benefits package.

"Now that you mention it," Ivan said, still twirling the shovel in his hand as if it were a scythe, "I did overhear something about a strike when I escorted my last appointment to the other side. They even had signs."

Well, then, we should leave well enough alone. We wouldn't want to cross any picket lines, would we? Remember, we're union friendly.

"I'm really trying to keep up with all this witch drama, but why would your Aunt Rowena still be using the Ouija board if no one on the other side is willing to help?" Heidi asked to anyone who would have the answer...which was no one. "Isn't that why you thought it was all taken care of, Ms. M?"

"I'll admit that I was a bit taken aback to find out that Ted saw Aunt Rowena here a couple of hours ago," my mother confessed, her worried gaze reluctantly landing on one of the crypts in front of us. "I'd honestly thought I'd taken care of our little afterlife issue."

I sighed in acceptance, because my mother actually thought she'd been doing something good for me and the residents of Paramour Bay. She'd been so against me moving here, and this entire time I thought she'd been devising some plan to get me to leave everything behind. Instead, she wanted to embrace this town once again as her own.

What just happened? Did we enter The Twilight Zone *or something? It sounded as if you were okay with your mother moving here, marrying my BFF, and basically invading our lives forever. I knew it. I've gone without my edibles for too long, and now I'm hallucinating. Call an ambulance.*

"...can't do something like that without ramifications. I should know, considering I tried to conduct a séance by myself early this summer. I thought I was the reason one of these crypts had a missing body. We need to stop taking chances before someone really gets hurt."

Oy vey. Leave it to Tweedledee and Tweedledum to make an appearance now.

The sound of Rye's voice had all of us turning to face the Watson family crypt. He was holding a flashlight underneath his arm, shutting the heavy wooden door firmly into place after Aunt Rowena exited the crypt. The crow that had been sitting on top of the small structure, ever so watchful, spread its wings and flew away, as if its job of overseeing the burial ground was done.

Aunt Rowena was carrying the bag that Ted had mentioned over her shoulder, and I had no doubt that she was lugging Gertie's Ouija board inside. Why had Aunt Rowena needed to use that particular board, and why did she feel that the help of our ancestors was needed to defeat the other faction?

"Good evening, Miss Marigold and Mr. Dolgiram," Ivan greeted, causing both Aunt Rowena and Rye to look like deer caught in headlights. "I take it that the two of you are done muddling up my job stats. I don't appreciate my numbers being skewed for my supervisor."

I know how you feel, Mr. Ivan. I truly do.

"Shame," Ted said with a shake of his head.

"Regina, I thought I had your word that nothing would be said to Raven," Aunt Rowena exclaimed, stepping forward with her head tilted in defiance. "This is quite the crowd you gathered round."

"Aunt Rowena, you know very well that Mom and I want no part of this war you've started. Why would you put the residents of Paramour Bay at risk?"

I closed the distance between us, grateful when Leo edged closer to be by my side. I'd motioned for Heidi to go stand next to Ivan and Ted, though she chose Ted's other side so that she maintained a bit of distance between her and the grim reaper. My mother joined me and Leo, making a barrier that Aunt Rowena wouldn't be able to get around without first answering for what she'd done…but she hadn't been inside that crypt all alone.

Don't get all mushy on me about standing by your side. I'm going to use that shovel to knock the Wicked Witch of Windsor over the head if she so much as mentions the toad spell.

"Rye, this is your town, too," I declared in disappointment. "These residents believe you are one of them, yet you still helped Aunt Rowena thin the veil enough to allow spirits to cross. How could you do that and then lie to my face?"

Hey, did you take a Guilt Trip 101 lesson from your mother? That was pretty good.

"It wasn't like that, Raven." Rye took the flashlight that he'd had tucked underneath his arm, turning it off now that the moon was providing enough light for us to see one another. His dark gaze seemed genuinely sorry for how far this ghost-invasion had gotten in the span of two days. "I honestly didn't know why the sightings were happening until I realized that the Ouija board I'd borrowed from Gertie wasn't in the window of the bakery. I'd promised Bree that I would help her decorate, and Gertie's Ouija board was the perfect centerpiece. Turns out that Gertie's great-great-grandmother was gifted, though more of a hedge witch."

I'd blame this one on my memory issues, but this is all new to me. I think.

"A medium or seer," I deduced, finally understanding why that particular Ouija board was so important in contacting our ancestors. "That still doesn't explain why you wouldn't have come to me. We could have stopped this before half the town saw their dead relatives, Rye."

"You don't get it, Raven. We're eventually going to have to pick a side," Rye said with a sad shake of his head. "And I'll always choose the woman who saved me from the streets when I had nowhere else to go."

Aunt Rowena smiled, though for some reason it didn't meet

her eyes.

I don't care. Can I use the shovel now?

"Leo, I'm very, very good at my craft," Aunt Rowena announced in retaliation, causing my mother to come to Leo's defense.

"You touch a strand of fur on that familiar's back, and we'll see who is better at their craft," my mother warned, to the surprise of us all.

Ohhh. I get it. This is a dream sequence. I'm sleeping, aren't I?

My mother pursed her red lips, tilting her head very similar to that of Aunt Rowena's stance. This was no dream, and it appeared that my mother was very confident with the decision to move back home.

Okay, that's it. I'm done. I have no idea how to act, what to say, or even how to feel. The only constant in my life is Skippy and his plans for world domination. Go figure.

"I've made many mistakes in my life, but I'm doing my best to make amends now. My mother might have been excommunicated from your dysfunctional coven, but she also wasn't exactly heartbroken to start anew. From what we've seen and heard these past two days, our entire ancestral line decided against joining either side of this war that is brewing within your broken coven. My daughter and I are going to follow their lead and declare Paramour Bay off limits."

I really, really need my edibles.

"I wish it were that easy, my dear niece," Aunt Rowena announced with disappointment. "You may think I put the citizens of Paramour Bay in danger with my need to contact the other side, but I did what was best for our family. You may not want to hear this, but I am the matriarch of the Marigold family. It is my duty to protect our lineage, and I will continue to do so on my own terms. I will be the one who unites the coven back together under one family name."

I can see everyone is hesitant to say this, but if that's the case...we're all doomed.

I'd been watching the exchange between my mother and Aunt Rowena. There was more than met the eye with this war between the factions. I could see the uneasiness in Rye's stature that he might very well be aware of the truth, while my mother and I were being kept in the dark. Aunt Rowena was going on and on about how the responsibility fell on the weight of her shoulders, yet there was something she was purposefully keeping from us.

"If that was true, Aunt Rowena, then Nan and our ancestors would have fallen in line behind you."

Aunt Rowena pursed her lips in that Marigold fashion, purposefully reaching into the bag that hung from her shoulder. She pulled out Gertie's Ouija board and handed it over to me.

"I've done what I've come to do, and the veil is back in place. Granted, it is a bit thinner this time of year, but you'll be happy to know that every wandering spirit has returned to the afterlife," Aunt Rowena declared haughtily, as if we should all be grateful for something that was entirely her fault to begin with. "We'll bid you goodnight and a joyous All Hallows' Eve."

"No."

Raven, I'm not entirely comfortable with you antagonizing the very woman who has threatened to turn me into a toad on more than one occasion.

"I beg your pardon?" Aunt Rowena did the Marigold brow arch that normally would have had me rethinking my directive. Yet I stood in front of her with family and friends who supported me in keeping this town safe from harm. "Raven, I simply reached out to our ancestors. There was no crime committed here, no one was harmed, and everything was made right. This isn't one of your mysteries where someone ends up going to jail."

I changed my mind. Regina, please tell me you know the toad spell. I give you permission to unleash all the warts at your disposal.

"You're right, Aunt Rowena," I agreed, confidence that had been gained over the last year flowing through me. The energy in my palm had begun spiraling as it began piercing my skin, but there was no need to resort to that particular offensive measure just yet. "You aren't going to end up in jail for reaching out to our ancestors. You will, however, have to answer to me if you ever so much as consider practicing magic in this town again without first running it by me."

My mother reached over and grabbed ahold of my arm. At first, I thought she was going to say I'd taken things too far, but instead she squeezed my forearm in support. She'd finally accepted that this was my place in life, and she would stand by me from this point forward. Heidi did the same on the other side of me, and I could feel Ted come to stand behind me in a show of solidarity.

"This place is our home, and these residents are our family," I continued, thinking back over the year that had changed not only my way of life, but who I was: from an insecure girl in my twenties to a woman who was now in her thirties. "I suggest you leave for Windsor first thing in the morning. You're not welcome here."

Rye would have argued, but Aunt Rowena put a hand up to stop him. She regarded me quietly, but I got the sense that she'd accepted my directive. Neither my mother nor I were going to get involved in coven business unless the war threatened our home.

"Fine." Aunt Rowena even gave a slight nod, as if she respected my stance. I wasn't sure that was the case, but at least she would be leaving town before anyone could be hurt by her desire to seek help from our ancestors. "The renovations on my house should be completed tomorrow, and I will drive back to Windsor. Know this, Raven. There are factors at play that involve our family…and I do mean all of us. I cannot guarantee that this war will not spill over into your lives, but I will do my best to keep the three of you out of it. Rye, would you please escort me back to the house?"

Isn't it nice that the Wicked Witch of Windsor included me in that promise?

"I think she was referring to Heidi," my mother murmured as we all stared after Aunt Rowena and Rye as they began to make their way toward the front of the cemetery. "I don't like that she's hiding things from us, Raven. We have a very big problem on our hands."

Yeah. The fact that the Wicked Witch of Windsor thinks I would help her do anything is a problem. Are you sure she meant Heidi and not me? I'm not cut out to be used as a weapon for war.

"I'm afraid you're right," I replied, having come to the same conclusion. "What do you think Aunt Rowena is hiding about our family?"

It must be a doozy if our ancestors had denied her request and basically gone on strike; that is, according to Ivan. If those already passed on to the other side wanted no part of this war, it stood to reason that we shouldn't either.

Spellblocked. It's a thing.

"I'm not sure, but I now understand why my life has brought me back here. Fate is fickle, Raven, but she always gets her way."

My mother had turned from the two walking away to focus

on me. Her emerald green eyes were so much like mine, only wiser. She'd never given up her craft, but she'd chosen to hide it for some reason and attempted to give me a normal life. Why? Was she keeping something from me in the same way that Aunt Rowena had been doing this last year?

In my experience, it's always better to ask those kinds of questions over edibles or a hit off my pipe.

"Mom, why was Aunt Rowena trying to contact our ancestors?"

"I honestly don't know, but I intend to find out." My mother held out her hands to both Heidi and me. We both gave her offer consideration before stepping forward and taking what she offered—a truce. "Heidi, you're like a daughter to me. Whether or not you were born a Marigold, you are part of this family. It's inevitable that we're going to be dragged into this war, so I'd say it's in our best interest to find out why. Are we in this together?"

Hey, Ivan. Do you need a helper? I think I might be out of work. I'll take catnip as payment, but it's got to be premium organic.

"You aren't out of work, Leo," I assured him with a light laugh, even knowing that we might be going up against something a lot bigger than our small group. "If anything, your responsibilities just doubled. You've got a new hedge witch to train."

Doubled? Does this mean my premium organic catnip supply doubles in payment? Keep talking, witches. You're speaking my language!

Chapter Eighteen

"MAYBE IT'S TIME we tell your mother that I know the truth," Liam said after giving an eight-year-old pirate a high five to go along with his snack-sized Snickers. "We'll tell her together after your birthday celebration."

Those of us who had been at the cemetery had made our way back to the tea shop, though Ted had gone down to Mindy's boutique so that he could spend some quality time with the mannequin he fancied. My mother and Beetle were manning the table with the tea samples for the adults, while Liam and I were at the other high-top table with candy for the children. Heidi's office wasn't on River Bay, so she'd gone across the street to assist Trixie with the diner's apple bob. As for Leo, he was just finishing up the edible treats that Beetle had somehow made into the shapes of jack o'lantern cookies.

Everything had gone back to normal in our small town, yet it hadn't.

"I agree that we need to tell my mother, but let's make that a private conversation at the cottage," I said softly, not wanting my voice to carry the ten feet to where the second table was positioned by the door. "I'm still wrapping my head around everything that happened tonight. I mean, Rye basically warned us that we would have no choice but to get involved with the Coven War at some point in the near future. I do believe that

Aunt Rowena wants to keep us out of it, but I'm afraid we're going to find that it's out of our hands. And I'm not so sure she's keeping us in the dark for completely altruistic reasons."

Altruistic and the Wicked Witch of Windsor can't be used in the same sentence, Raven. There's a dictionary on your phone. They're juxtaposed. While you're at it, you'll also find her picture in front of a word that rhymes with witch.

Leo had been in rare form since we'd gotten back to the tea shop, but that's how he dealt with stress—snarkiness. At least, when his apprehension didn't affect his memory.

There was one last group of children making their way toward us with their parents in tow. After that, we'd begin to clean up and head over to the pub, where everyone was invited to an All Hallows' Eve birthday celebration. I was truly looking forward to celebrating this past year, where I'd come into my own and grown as a woman, but our run-in with Aunt Rowena took a bit of joy out of the festivities. I'd most likely made an enemy out of my own great-aunt.

"Hey, Beetle," Liam called out, surprising both me and Leo. "Could you finish handing out the candy in this bowl? We'll be right back."

Liam took me by the hand and led me away from the high-top table through the glass door and back into the tea shop. I'd dimmed the lights inside so that the strings of orange pumpkins glowed brighter, and I wish I was in the mood to enjoy the ambiance. It was very hard to get into the festivities when there was a cloud of supernatural doom hanging over our heads.

Welcome to my world.

Leo had decided to join us, but Liam didn't seem to mind. As a matter of fact, Liam had pulled a small, wrapped present out from what seemed like nowhere by the time I'd turned around to face him. I had no idea where he'd hid it all this time, but a smile graced my lips. This intimate moment was just what I needed after the last two days.

I already feel a hairball at the back of my throat, but the antici-pation is too much. I can't leave now, so I'll just have to suffer through. What are you waiting for? Open it. Maybe it's the deed to a catnip farm in Alaska. You could rake in the money while I perform quality and product testing. A win-win for both of us.

"Liam," I whispered, covering my heart with my hands. The present was wrapped with orange paper that had printed black cats, flying bats, and several moons positioned strategically around the small box. A black ribbon with orange sparkles was impeccably crooked, and I wouldn't have had it any other way. "It's perfect."

"You haven't even opened it," Liam said with a chuckle, handing it over while looking up at the overhead light. "We need more light."

"No," I replied softly, tugging on the ribbon. "I want to remember this moment exactly like this."

It's best to remain in the shadows. One never knows if the Wick-ed Witch of Windsor has a scout or if Skippy sent one of his ninja squirrels to keep an eye on my anti-squirrelpocalypse operation. I've left directions for my secret plan underneath my cat bed.

Liam patiently waited for me to remove the wrapping paper. I didn't want to rip it, having every intention of saving the paper and ribbon to be cherished. By the time I'd lifted off the lid, I'd been confident that it was some type of jewelry box. What I found was more profound and heartfelt than I could ever have imagined.

"Liam, it's beautiful," I whispered in awe, unable to reach inside for my present just yet.

Liam finally did it for me, pulling out a black tourmaline pendent surrounded by heavy silver filigree. I'd been wanting one for a while now, but I just hadn't gotten around to buying one for myself. This particular gem was known for its protection elements, but this one seemed to glow with an inner light all its own.

"You mentioned wanting a black tourmaline to carry with you, so I found this one wrapped in silver. It's an antique dating back to Salem in the middle 1600s. It was owned by the Good family. It even came with a letter documenting its legacy all the way back to Sarah Good." Liam indicated for me to turn around, so I set the box next to the wrapping paper and ribbon I'd laid next to a porcelain tea set. I lifted my hair so that it would be easier for him to clasp the necklace. "Who would have guessed that it might come in handy in the immediate future?"

"So, you're a believer now?" I teased, already knowing that I'd convinced him that the supernatural existed.

"Raven," Liam said softly, waiting to finish what he intended to say until I'd turned around to face him. "I've always believed in your magic."

He cradled my cheek as he leaned down to kiss me. His warm lips pressed to mine as the heat of the crystal reassured me that it was offering up its protection. I would reciprocate and make sure that Liam had his own protection, maybe even going so far as to do a protection spell of some sort. I couldn't have him getting hurt by my own family.

Hairball! I tried to give you some privacy, but the good ol' sheriff had to ruin it with that cheesy line. Don't tell him, though. I owe him one for my fast recovery this morning.

"Thank you, Liam," I murmured against his lips, giving him one more kiss before pulling away. I looked down at the black tourmaline encased in the hand-carved silver, recognizing the significance of the gift as more than just a present. It was an affirmation that Liam accepted me for me. That meant he accepted Leo, as well. "It's perfect. Let me grab my sweater from the back room. It's getting cold, and this witch outfit doesn't offer me much warmth."

I quickly made my way through the ivory-colored fairy beads, flipping the light switch so that I wasn't fumbling around in the dark. I'd learned to always keep a sweater back here for those days the temperature had big swings, which was often with the coastal breeze coming in off the water.

Speaking of the change in weather, I'm taking tomorrow off. Since we don't know when the Wicked Witch of Windsor plans to ruin our lives with her little war, I'm dedicating the next couple of weeks to defeating the squirrelpocalypse. Don't tell Skippy, but I do miss our feud during the winter months. At least I'll have the weekly poker games to look forward to and get me through until the spring.

"I'm sure Skippy misses you, too," I reassured Leo, the doom and gloom ambiance having lifted the moment Liam had pulled me inside the tea shop. There was nothing for me to do about this war between the factions of the coven, and I had a birthday to celebrate with my family and friends. "You can take the entire day and—"

Something had floated to the ground when I'd taken my sweater off the stool I'd set it on earlier. It was a small piece of paper. I leaned down to pick it up, believing it was a receipt that I hadn't properly filed away. Upon closer inspection, the palm of my right hand began to fill with warmth.

No, it didn't. You're mistaken. Throw that piece of paper into the trashcan right now, Raven.

"Leo, it's a message," I whispered in disbelief. We'd both

wondered why Nan hadn't paid us a visit when everyone else seemed to call on their loved ones after Aunt Rowena had pierced the veil. After hearing from her that the Marigold ancestors had basically gone on strike and refused to speak with her, we'd all assumed that was the reason Nan had stayed far away from us. There was no mistaking her handwriting, though. "It's from Nan."

I blame the Wicked Witch of Windsor for this, you know. She's the reason my beloved Rosemary had to stay away from us. I bet that your grandmother knows the toad spell, and she could have shared it with you and your mother.

"Leo?"

Oh, there's that tone again. The one that tells me you're about to delay my heroic actions of bringing the squirrelpocalypse to a halt. Does my beloved Rosemary at least tell me how to handle two Marigolds at once? She must have left a manual behind or something.

"No manual, but she did write me a message—*you're the one.*"

Seriously? That's what my beloved Rosemary took the time to write while we were dealing with the Wicked Witch of Windsor? Wait just a bat's wing. You're the one for what? To stop the squirrelpocalypse?

"I don't know," I whispered in apprehension as I stared at the note. There was something ominous about being the one responsible for something I was basically in the dark over. I instinctively rested my right hand over my gift, thankful for Liam and his thoughtfulness. I might need this gemstone now more than ever. "I don't know, Leo, but we need to be prepared for anything. There is one more prophetic piece to the message...*wear the stone.*"

It's a good thing I fortified myself with some edibles. Okay, Raven. First things first—we need to prepare you a bug-out bag.

~ THE END ~

Find out who's been naughty or nice in the next snowbound whodunit of the Paramour Bay Mysteries by USA Today Bestselling Author Kennedy Layne...

kennedylayne.com/yuletide-blend.html

Stockings are hung by the chimney with care and visions of catnip dance in the air this yuletide season in Paramour Bay. The spirit of giving is in full swing, and the residents of this small coastal Connecticut town are finishing up their last minute holiday shopping.

Raven Marigold takes a break from minding the tea shop to enjoy the winter wonderland the council members have magically created in the middle of town square. The holiday festival has everything from a lighted Christmas tree to singing elves. Even good ol' St. Nick has shown up to hear the wish lists of excited children, but the jolliness in his ho-ho-ho disappears when one of his reindeer goes missing! Is this a reindeer-napping or has the precious animal just wandered off?

Grab a plate of sugar cookies and a glass of milk as Raven and the gang attempt to unwrap the next seasonal whodunit in order to save the cheer for a Merry Christmas this year!

Books by Kennedy Layne

Hex on Me Mysteries
If the Curse Fits
Cursing up the Wrong Tree
The Squeaky Ghost Gets the Curse
The Curse that Bites
Curse Me Under the Mistletoe

Paramour Bay Mysteries
Magical Blend
Bewitching Blend
Enchanting Blend
Haunting Blend
Charming Blend
Spellbinding Blend
Cryptic Blend
Broomstick Blend
Spirited Blend
Yuletide Blend

Office Roulette Series
Means (Office Roulette, Book One)
Motive (Office Roulette, Book Two)
Opportunity (Office Roulette, Book Three)

Keys to Love Series
Unlocking Fear (Keys to Love, Book One)
Unlocking Secrets (Keys to Love, Book Two)
Unlocking Lies (Keys to Love, Book Three)
Unlocking Shadows (Keys to Love, Book Four)
Unlocking Darkness (Keys to Love, Book Five)

Surviving Ashes Series
Essential Beginnings (Surviving Ashes, Book One)

Hidden Ashes (Surviving Ashes, Book Two)
Buried Flames (Surviving Ashes, Book Three)
Endless Flames (Surviving Ashes, Book Four)
Rising Flames (Surviving Ashes, Book Five)

CSA CASE FILES SERIES
Captured Innocence (CSA Case Files 1)
Sinful Resurrection (CSA Case Files 2)
Renewed Faith (CSA Case Files 3)
Campaign of Desire (CSA Case Files 4)
Internal Temptation (CSA Case Files 5)
Radiant Surrender (CSA Case Files 6)
Redeem My Heart (CSA Case Files 7)
A Mission of Love (CSA Case Files 8)

RED STARR SERIES
Starr's Awakening(Red Starr, Book One)
Hearths of Fire (Red Starr, Book Two)
Targets Entangled (Red Starr, Book Three)
Igniting Passion (Red Starr, Book Four)
Untold Devotion (Red Starr, Book Five)
Fulfilling Promises (Red Starr, Book Six)
Fated Identity (Red Starr, Book Seven)
Red's Salvation (Red Starr, Book Eight)

THE SAFEGUARD SERIES
Brutal Obsession (The Safeguard Series, Book One)
Faithful Addiction (The Safeguard Series, Book Two)
Distant Illusions (The Safeguard Series, Book Three)
Casual Impressions (The Safeguard Series, Book Four)
Honest Intentions (The Safeguard Series, Book Five)
Deadly Premonitions (The Safeguard Series, Book Six)

ABOUT THE AUTHOR

First and foremost, I love life. I love that I'm a wife, mother, daughter, sister… and a writer.

I am one of the lucky women in this world who gets to do what makes them happy. As long as I have a cup of coffee (maybe two or three) and my laptop, the stories evolve themselves and I try to do them justice. I draw my inspiration from a retired Marine Master Sergeant that swept me off of my feet and has drawn me into a world that fulfills all of my deepest and darkest desires. Erotic romance, military men, intrigue, with a little bit of kinky chili pepper (his recipe), fill my head and there is nothing more satisfying than making the hero and heroine fulfill their destinies.

Thank you for having joined me on their journeys…

Email: kennedylayneauthor@gmail.com

Facebook: facebook.com/kennedy.layne.94

Twitter: twitter.com/KennedyL_Author

Website: www.kennedylayne.com

Newsletter: www.kennedylayne.com/aboutnewsletter.html